A CERTAIN ISLAND

drawings by **JOHN PIMLOTT**

A CERTAIN ISLAND

by Robert Murphy

M Evans
Lanham • New York • Boulder • Toronto • Plymouth, UK

M. Evans
An imprint of The Rowman & Littlefield Publishing Group, Inc.
4501 Forbes Boulevard, Suite 200, Lanham, Maryland 20706
http://www.rlpgtrade.com

10 Thornbury Road, Plymouth PL6 7PP, United Kingdom

Distributed by National Book Network

First Rowman & Littlefield paperback edition 2014

British Library Cataloguing in Publication Information Available

Library of Congress Cataloging-in-Publication Data Available

ISBN 13: 978-1-59077-324-6 (pbk: alk. paper)

The paper used in this publication meets the minimum requirements of American National Standard for Information Sciences—Permanence of Paper for Printed Library Materials, ANSI/NISO Z39.48-1992.

Printed in the United States of America

Howbeit we must be cast upon a certain island.

ACTS 27:26

The small expedition to Laysan Island with which this novel is concerned actually took place. The island can be found on the map at the location given, and the background of history and birdlife is true. But the characters and events set forth are imaginary. The young man who made the trip bears some outward resemblance to Alfred M. Bailey, who is now the Director of the Denver Museum of Natural History. Dr. Bailey was born in Iowa and several of his boyhood adventures suggested a few of the things that occur in the book, but that is all. Dr. Bailey is not Geordie nor were Geordie's problems his, any more than the other characters in the novel are the actual people who went to Laysan.

When I was first thinking of the book, I went to see Dr. Bailey. He and his family were most hospitable and generous in providing me with notes, diaries and museum publications, some of which are now out of print, containing Dr. Bailey's articles and pictures relative to the trip he had made so long ago. Without this help I doubt that the skeleton of A CERTAIN ISLAND would ever have been formed, and I am most grateful to them all.

Robert Murphy
Westtown, Pennsylvania

A CERTAIN ISLAND

ONE

His name was George Sutton and they called him Geordie; there was a Geordie in every generation because the family, being sober fellows and studious in the main, held to a romantic and quixotic affection for a remote ancestor named Geordie MacFarlane, "Old Geordie," a Highland Scot who had lost his head because of his enterprise with a claymore in support of Bonnie Prince Charlie in the '45. There was a sort of wistfulness in this affection, as though each succeeding generation held the hope of another wild and reckless son who would shake off the pale cast of thought, the family's habit of carefully considering every decision, in the wholehearted pursuit of an immoderate illusion. None of them had ever admitted that if such a son appeared it would horrify them.

By the end of the 19th century there had been none and the prospect still wasn't very bright, for the family was established in Iowa by this time and was producing lawyers; as the century came near its end our Geordie appeared and he didn't seem a likely candidate either. A tall, thin, dark-haired boy with a slow, engaging grin, he was more interested in the wildlife of the prairie sloughs and along the muddy Iowa River than he was in Blackstone or anybody like him. Not that he was a poor student; his grades had always been good enough to encourage a lenient attitude on the part of his father, but the lenient time was about over.

"Here he is," his father said to his mother toward the end of that summer, "about to go into his first year of college, and he'd still rather sit in a swamp than in a library. Where does he get such tastes? When he was in grammar school it was understandable, and probably good for him. The exercise, and that sort of thing. And a certain amount of self-reliance as well. But, I must say . . ."

"He's been reading Darwin," his mother said. "I found the book under his bed."

His father snorted, a method of expressing himself that wasn't characteristic of him; he usually took a reasonable and even judicious tone. "That wretched man," he said with distaste. "If they'd shaved him he'd have looked more like a monkey than he did. Not that I think," he went on quickly, "that his theories are stupid. They are not. They have a good deal to recommend them, despite the uproar that they have caused. But Geordie will addle his brains with such stuff at his age. It's time he began to read a little law. I do think I've been quite patient with the boy, Lavinia, and it seems to me that it's high time we began to make him understand that his future will be ill-served by continuing to run the woods and little else."

There was a short silence in the high-ceilinged living-room. Lavinia Sutton, dark haired, with beautiful dark eyes in an oval face, had been sitting with her hands in her lap, looking at the Turkish carpet while her husband talked; she stood up, walked over to him, and put her hands on his shoulders. "Did you always want to be a lawyer, Alfred?" she asked. "From a little boy?"

"My father was a lawyer, and so was his father. I suppose it was natural that I wanted to be one."

"But did you really want to be one? Did you have a vocation, and burrow into your father's library before you went to that eastern college?"

She smiled at him, attempting to get a lighter tone into the discussion, for she had worried ever since the spring when his impatience had begun to show.

"Yes," he said, answering her question but not her smile. "Listening to my father talk about the law, I saw a sort of . . . of beauty in it, reasonable and orderly. What else is there here for him, Lavinia?" he asked, with great seriousness. "He'll never be a doctor; I'm sure he wouldn't be a good farmer or a storekeeper. If he keeps going as he is now, he'll end up like that dirty old Possum Boniface, who's always in my office to be got off some charge or other. *That* I will not have."

Lavinia Sutton fell back a step, and her hands dropped to her sides. "Oh, Alfred!" she said. "Surely you don't think . . . You can't be serious. Alfred, he's so young!"

"When I was his age . . ." he began, and stopped and made an unhappy gesture with one hand. "Maybe I've shown my impatience. I'm sorry. I'll try not to do it again. Now I've got to go out and see Judge Meadows."

He kissed her, a little formally, turned, and started for the hall. She watched him go, seeing the straight back, the hair beginning to show a frost of gray, the carriage that the town knew and respected; she knew that Geordie respected him as well, perhaps too much, and was therefore in his shadow. She sighed.

While Geordie's father was talking about Possum Boniface, Geordie himself was sitting in a boat a few miles away with Possum himself. How he had got there was none of his own doing; he had been fishing from the riverbank with his cane pole held by a forked stick, stretched out in luxurious idleness in the sun and staring dreamily at his cork when Possum had come along in his scarred old boat, and backing it into the bank had invited Geordie to join him.

"I could do with a mite of help, boy," Possum said. "Climb in, and give me a hand."

"Sure," Geordie said. "Wait until I put my pole on the bank."

He knew Possum and had often stopped by Possum's shack a little further up the river for a word about where the ducks might be or other such matters, for Possum was always poking about and kept a sharp eye on the activities of what he called "the varmints." He was a hairy old man, always grimy, who lived alone in a monumental clutter. His horny feet were bare, as they always were until frost, his unshaven chin was stained with tobacco juice, and—to put a point on it—he smelled; he lived out of a bottle and off the country and consequently paid no attention to existing game laws or property lines, but aside from this idiosyncrasy there was no evil in him.

Geordie wrapped his line around the pole, hid the pole in the brush, and climbed aboard. He knew that Possum always had fish and hoped that the secret of this abundance might be revealed. He grinned at Possum, for Possum amused him; the old man's life was so different from the lives of the other people Geordie knew, so uncomplicated and empty of possessions that had to be eternally cared for, that he was a pleasant change occasionally. He wasn't a heroic figure, but he was free. "What's up?" Geordie asked.

"I need you to row," Possum said. "I aim to get a bait of fish." They changed places in the boat, and when Geordie had the oars Possum pointed to a backwater a hundred yards downstream with a stump sticking above the surface on the edge of it. "Row down there, and hang on to that stump."

Geordie eased the boat downstream, wondering how they were going to fish, for there weren't any poles or hand-lines visible. He didn't have to wonder long, for Possum reached under his seat, pulled out a box, and out of the box brought a stick of dynamite and broke it calmly in half. Geordie's jaw dropped a little; he had often heard of the spectacular effects of dynamite, and he knew that dynamiting fish was illegal. He was aware that he should put himself ashore and bow out at once, but the prospect was too exciting; he watched with a sort of horrified fascination as Possum put a cap and fuse on the dynamite, wrapped it and a stone in a piece of oiled paper, and tied everything up with a piece of fishing line from his pocket.

They had drifted past the stump by that time, and Geordie rowed back and took hold of it. Possum stood up, looked up and down the river to see if the coast was clear, struck a match on the seat of his pants, and touched it to the fuse. The fuse began to sizzle; Possum held the package for a moment and then threw it toward the backwater. A loop in the string caught on his thumb, and the dynamite swung around and fell into the boat.

Geordie's hair stood up and a paralysis seized him; he sat staring at the fuse, and couldn't have moved to save his life. Possum started to jump overboard, changed his mind, whirled about, and because his legs were crossed fell toward the dynamite. The boat rocked wildly; Possum's reaching hand fell two inches short, and he humped himself desperately along the floorboards, reached the dynamite, managed to half stand up, and threw the package toward the backwater. "Git!" he shouted, turning to Geordie. "Git!"

Geordie, hanging onto the heaving boat, was galvanized into action, and dug the oars desperately into the water. Possum scuttled forward and took the oars too and the pair of them pulled until their muscles cracked, splashing water all about. The boat began to move slowly; they got in about four strokes when the dynamite let go with a roar, concussion thumped the boat, and a column of water rose into the air. This frightened them so that they feathered the oars; Geordie fell backwards and Possum fell on top of him. The waves caused by the explosion almost capsized them, and after lying in terror for a moment they untangled themselves and sat up groggily.

The water was flattening out and a number of fish were belly up on the surface among fragments of trash from the bottom. They both stared at the scene for a moment, and then Possum pushed Geordie toward the bow, took the oars himself, and rowed into midstream. A long reach opened to the south, and at the far end of it they saw a boat. Possum muttered something to himself, straightened up to get a better look at it, and then bent to the oars and rowed rapidly to the point where he had picked Geordie up. He turned into shore, and Geordie scrambled out. Standing shakily on the bank, he exchanged a long look with Possum, who now seemed impatient to be gone.

"You going to collect the fish?" he asked.

"Heck with the fish," Possum said. A strange, greenish pallor had appeared on his unshaven face. "You can have 'em. I swallered my chaw, and I got to go home for my tonic." His jaw was shaking, and after abstractedly noting this Geordie watched him as he dug in the oars and made rapidly for a bend in the river and disappeared.

The boy sat down on the bank, drew a long breath, and blew it out again. He raised a hand to his own jaw, to see whether it was shaking like Possum's, couldn't find it was, and felt proud of himself. As he recalled the sequence of events fragmentary pictures of what he had seen as they scrambled about came to him, and then he began to laugh. He laughed immoderately, a little lightheaded from relief, and when it was over he shook his head, looked up at the sky that he might never have seen again, and then lowered his head. There was a boat lying a few feet off the bank with a man sitting in it. It startled him so that he jumped; he hadn't heard it, or noticed it coming up.

The man was facing him, resting on his oars. He was a big man, well-muscled, bareheaded, dressed in khaki pants and shirt, with a square, sunburnt, unsmiling face; his gray eyes were like the eyes of a teacher who is trying to get to the bottom of some piece of classroom deviltry. Geordie stared at him, uneasy now and still startled by his sudden appearance.

"Did you see a boat with two people in it come by here, boy?" he asked.

"No, sir," Geordie said, and then recalled the other boat they had seen far down the reach. Maybe, he thought with a sinking feeling, it was the game warden. His throat tightened up, and he swallowed. He shook his head. "No, sir," he said again.

"Did you hear a noise?"

Geordie was a truthful boy, but he was frightened; he had heard many of his father's stories of malefactors being apprehended and going to jail, and he knew very well his father's feelings about them. He wanted to tell the truth and try to explain his innocence, but couldn't; all he could think of was his father's reaction if the man found him out and took him to his father's office. He was going to have to lie his way out of the situation. He swallowed again. "Yes, sir," he said. "I heard a noise. It was sort of like an explosion."

"H'm," the man said, and considered him. Then he said, suddenly: "You weren't in that boat?"

"No, sir," Geordie said, and felt himself beginning to shake. "I didn't see a boat."

"What's your name?"

"Geordie Sutton," Geordie said.

"Alfred Sutton's boy?"

"Yes, sir," Geordie said, and felt a trickle of perspiration begin to take its way down his back.

The man's eyebrows went up, and he nodded. There seemed to be a sudden relaxation of the tension in him, the feeling that he was about to pounce was lightened; the mysterious power of Alfred Sutton's name upon him was amazing. Geordie dared to take a full breath.

"What were you doing here, Geordie?" the man asked, in a tone that sounded almost friendly.

"I was fishing," Geordie said. "I'd just put my pole away." He was suddenly released from the immobility that had held him. "See?" he asked, and ran back to the brush where he had hid the pole. He got down on his knees and groped in the brush, his hands still shaking, and finally brought out the pole. "See?" he asked again, holding it up. "I was just going home."

"You were laughing like a loon."

"Yes, sir," Geordie said. "I . . ." No reason why he had been laughing like a loon came into his head, and he was sensible enough not to try to fumble about for one. "Yes, sir, I was."

The man looked at him for a long moment, nodded, and dipped the oars. Geordie watched him pull away, filled with a relief so intense that it was almost painful. The boat rounded the point and vanished. Geordie stared at the empty water for a few seconds, let out a long breath, and hid the pole again. He sat down beside it until the trembling in him stopped, stood up, and walked through the riverside brush to the narrow dirt road and got on his bicycle and headed home.

He was still a little light-headed with relief at having got off so lightly after his first brush with the law as he came into the familiar quiet, tree-lined streets with their well-spaced houses and stables in the rear, the lawns bright with early fall flowers in the flowerbeds, solid, staid, and respectable; in this reassuring atmosphere he began to settle down. His recent adventure, from the business with the dynamite to the encounter with the warden, began to seem improbable and far away, as though it had happened a long time ago and even to someone else, a story that he had heard and not been involved in himself.

He came to his own tree-lined driveway and turned in. The big wooden house, painted white, with a shingled cupola and a porte-cochere, was set well back from the street; there was a pretty little white stable behind it. The lawn beneath the trees was dappled with afternoon sunlight. It was a good house, one of the best in town, and rather impressive; it had been built by a real estate promoter who had made a good deal of money selling prairie farmland to immigrants from the East, land-hungry people who had heard of the richness of the prairie earth. Some of the land had been drained marshes that hadn't worked out very well for farming, and there had been litigation and other unpleasantness that had finally resulted in the promoter's moving away.

Geordie had been born in the house several years after his father had bought it, and his memories began with the big, high, airy rooms through which he still moved. His life in it had been pleasant, a typical Midwestern boyhood, provincial and easygoing, surrounded with plenty of open country, little conflict or big-city excitement, and with people from the University or the professions in the main. His father was regarded as the town's best lawyer, had a fine practice, and would probably end up as a judge. His bent was intellectual rather than physical; he had never been an outdoorsman and secretly thought (despite a number of his friends who seemed to enjoy outdoor life) that anyone who would arise in the middle of the night to go slopping around a duck marsh or march about to shoot wild birds much like chickens was somewhat of a fool.

He was proud of his intelligence and his position, and wanted his son to follow in his footsteps; it worried him that Geordie seemed to be headed for a life that would be fulfilled with an enterprise on the level of taxidermy or veterinary medicine—"horse doctoring"—or some similar messy business.

Geordie cycled through the porte-cochere and on to the stable where Laverty, the man of all work, was washing the Packard. Laverty, an old Irishman who looked a little like a monkey and had a fringe of ginger whiskers, was in a bad humor; he loved horses, the feel of good leather, and the delicate lines of fine coachwork, and always grew morose when he had to deal with the new-fangled devices that he called "machines." He looked up when Geordie appeared, spat on a fender to express his contempt of the car, and washed the spittle off with the hose. "Ah, now," he said. "The young frontiersman hisself. And what might you have been up to?"

Geordie almost told him, for Laverty in his better moments was full of tales of poaching in the old country and the new, but caught himself in time; he had found by bitter experience that a misguided word to Laverty found its way to Ingrid the cook and from there to his mother. "I've been fishing," he said.

"And where might the fish be? Do we all starve because Your Honor's after fallin' asleep by the river?"

"Do you think my name is Laverty?" asked Geordie, and ran around to the other side of the car before Laverty could turn the hose on him. He put the bicycle away, and watching his chance ran for the house; the nozzle turned his way, but the stream fell short.

Ingrid wasn't in the kitchen, and by the clock it was an hour until dinner; he went up the back stairs to his room. It was at the rear of the house, somewhat off by itself, a big, bright, corner room with four windows. There was an oval rag rug on the floor, Geordie had made bookcases that lined one wall, and there was a big, old desk of his father's with a green-shaded student's lamp, a muskrat's skull, a badly stuffed Wilson's phalarope, a pad, and a small Navajo pot full of pencils on it, a double bed covered with an India print, and three upholstered chairs. A double-barreled shotgun stood in a corner with a baseball bat, and the pictures around the walls were of birds and animals. Most of them were animals and birds of other countries—Africa, India, and the Arctic, places remote and mysterious; Geordie was a great reader of books about these places, and longed in an abstract way to visit them.

As he often did when he came into the room, he withdrew from the rest of the house, the people around him, and the things that he had been doing recently. He paused in the middle of the room and looked around, unseeing, for this was the place where he came to detach himself from his everyday life and, in effect, live the clouded life of the future.

This life, or the fantasies that made it up, weren't very specific, for he didn't know yet what he wanted to do. In his daydreams he wandered in far places, leading scientific expeditions into exotic jungles; sometimes he was being congratulated by presidents of learned societies for triumphs that he couldn't recall, and occasionally these men looked like his father. He was always pleased when they did, but in any case the visions would finally fade away and he would be in his room again, tingling and excited by the strangeness and color of them, but wondering for a time afterward what he had done to deserve the honors heaped upon him. Lately he had come to the point where the adventures weren't sufficient because of their inconclusiveness; he was beginning to realize in a hazy way that merely wandering about even in the most exotic situations didn't satisfy him.

For the past few months he had been groping about, trying various things; the stuffing of a few birds, which hadn't seemed to please his father very much, was one of them. He had even tried to write poetry, but it had all sounded so much like either *The Rubaiyat* or *The Idylls Of The King* (one he read in school, and the other he happened upon by himself) that he was discouraged by it. He wanted it to sound like himself, but when he sat down in front of a blank page and faced the question of what to say he couldn't find an answer and wound up echoing the others.

Today, when he got into this room where he was cut off from the outside world, in which just living was sufficient and the activity of living was satisfying, he wanted more than ever to find something that would give his inner life direction. This time his dissatisfaction was closer to the surface than it had ever been before. Perhaps the shaking up that the affair with Possum and then the game warden had given him was responsible, for he felt guilty about them even though he hadn't admitted it to himself, and this guilt made him more dissatisfied with his reveries than usual.

He stood looking at the phalarope. The light was waning in the room, and somehow the shadowed shape of the bird seemed to hold a clue to the future, a clue to an answer that wouldn't come clear. This feeling lasted but a moment; it popped into his head and was gone, a fugitive thing like a sound that one thinks he has heard but isn't sure, and it puzzled Geordie. How *could* it mean anything, especially about the future? He walked over and picked it up.

When it was in his hand, hard and dry, he began remembering. He had shot it in the spring, and as he recalled seeing the bird, one of three, falling into the grass of the marsh, the previous seasons of the year now passing began to come back to him.

TWO

The impetus to stuff the phalarope, which was the reason why it had been shot, had come during the winter. It was then that he had found an advertisement that had caught his eye in one of the five-cent magazines that circulated among the boys of the class. BE A TAXIDERMIST, it said, in big, black letters. FIND FUN AND PROFIT IN THIS FASCINATING HOBBY. There was a picture of a young man, surrounded with mounted birds and animals in lifelike poses, pointing them out to another young man who seemed greatly impressed by the products of his skill and industry. Geordie had never thought of stuffing anything, for most of the time in his comings and goings he was surrounded by wildlife; the banks of the river and the marshes were lively with animals and nesting birds in the summer and vast numbers of migrating birds in the spring and fall. The great waterfowl migrations were still spectacular; they had not at that time been greatly reduced, and although market hunting was whittling down the clouds of ducks and shorebirds there were still immense numbers of them.

Seeing them alive and moving in great skeins across the sky, being out where they were and in the midst of them, had been enough for Geordie in the several winters that he had been allowed to go about and hunt. These had been mild winters, when he could get out; but the last winter, the one when the advertisement found him, had been a bad one. It closed in early with a series of storms, a lot of snow, and the howling, bitter cold such as only the prairie country can produce, and he had been held away from his usual trips. The hardy creatures that stayed in mild winters fled; they couldn't have been found even if he had been able to look for them.

He missed them, and he missed the trips. The long hours that he had formerly spent stalking a stray mallard or a pintail, trapping muskrats, hiding in a marsh for a possible shot, or exploring an island in the River had to be spent at home; snowball fights and what sledding could be had in a country where hills were low and infrequent weren't enough for him. It wasn't that he was antisocial; he got on well enough with other boys; it was just that he preferred, most of the time, to be out under the sky, out of town, among the birds and animals to watch and learn a little more about them. They were more interesting than people because they were more mysterious, forever changing with the seasons, infinite in their variety and curious in their actions, wary and hidden; and the vast sweep of the country had the same attraction to him that the vast sweep of the sea has to a sailor.

He missed all this so much in the short gloomy days when the wind buffeted the house that the advertisement caught him; if he couldn't be out where he wanted to be, this was a way to bring it home. He saw himself, like the man in the picture, surrounded with carefully mounted specimens. He picked up the magazine from the desk and went looking for his mother and found her in the kitchen with Ingrid, who was making pastry. Ingrid was a big, very fair, Danish girl; she had the tabletop covered with a great thin disc of dough and was buttering and folding and rolling it, and then doing these things again; the big warm kitchen was fragrant with the smell of spices and almonds and other things.

Geordie drew a deep breath and forgot the magazine for a moment. Sometimes, years later, in many strange corners of the world where the food was very bad and life was very uncomfortable, that wonderful fragrance would come to him for a moment and he would remember; possibly it was because it was connected with the advertisement that had been so important to him. Then he recalled the magazine again, and held it out. "Ma," he asked, "could I send the coupon?"

It seemed to Geordie that she looked at it for a long time, and her eyes narrowed a little as though she was thinking of something else. He began to feel very apprehensive, and then she nodded. "Why, yes, Geordie, if you want to. If you really want to. I'll do it for you, if you like."

The coupon brought more enticing literature, Geordie sent his money, and presently he had several books about taxidermy. They set forth the best way to skin birds and animals, how to treat the skins and mount them, how to make rugs and fur pieces, and listed supplies that were necessary. He paid little attention to the making of rugs and fur pieces but studied the rest with great seriousness and finally sent off for several tools and chemicals. He wanted to buy some glass eyes, but didn't know what to buy them for; that would have to wait until his subjects appeared. Now that he was ready to go to work there was nothing to work on, and finally he hunted up Laverty and found him in the harness room. Busy with a sponge and saddle soap, Laverty was feeling cheerful; there was a pot-bellied stove going full blast, and he was whistling "The Drummer Boy To The War Has Gone," working away on a harness with his sleeves rolled up.

"Ah, now," he said, pausing in his labors. "So it's something to stuff, is it? Belike you should be looking for a polar bear."

"They're a little big to start on," Geordie said, with a straight face.

"Not for a boyo with your insolence. They're not big enough."

"But Laverty, I've got to have something."

"There'll be plenty in the spring."

"I know, but I've got to practice before spring gets here."

"Ah, now."

"You can help me, if you will. Think, now."

Laverty grinned at him. "I could think better if I had a bun or two from the kitchen. That girl's been bakin' again."

"Will you really think of something if I snitch a pastry?"

"Buns and a little dram from His Worship's bottle. The one on the sideboard."

"Oh, no," Geordie said. The bottle was covered by a

law that he wouldn't break, a law as inflexible as those of

the Medes and Persians. "I can't."

"I'm thinkin' of a cat," Laverty said. "What could be better than a cat? A great black beast, black as Belial and twice as nasty, with a tail on him would be better on a lion. Ah, think what you could do with him."

Geordie was thinking, and could hardly stand still at the prospect of it; a dramatic and marvelous vision filled his mind's eye. "Where would you get it, Laverty?"

"I might tell you and I might not, right this minute, but don't be after worryin'. If I had the dram—"

"No," Geordie said. "Two buns?"

"Maybe for two buns, then. But the girl can't know of it, or she'll be tellin' the Missus they were took for Laverty, and him with so little pleasure in his life."

"All right," Geordie said, and took off for the house. He went in the front door and drifted toward the kitchen, at once innocent and casual but taking advantage of any available cover. There was silence in the kitchen but he flowed around the corner of the coat closet and crept in among the coats; by moving them gently aside he could see most of the kitchen. It was empty, and he crept into it, found the pastries in the cabinet, and grasped two of them. Just then there were footsteps on the back stairs. His line of escape to either door was cut off, and after a swift, desperate look around he ran behind the stove, which was set out a little from the wall, and crouched down. Ingrid came into the kitchen, said something under her breath, and shut the cabinet door, which he had left open; then she sat down on the chair beside the kitchen table. Geordie's heart sank; it was hot and cramped behind the stove, and there was no telling how long he would be there.

Very soon he began to perspire, and his cramped muscles began to twitch. Ingrid sat on. Time drew out, and perspiration trickled down Geordie's hide and tickled him. Having hidden himself, he couldn't emerge now with some fabrication or other; he thought bitterly that if he hadn't panicked he could have asked Ingrid for the pastry for himself. She would have given them to him; she always did.

More time went on, and Geordie was in despair; just as he thought he would either have to die or crawl out and be in disgrace, the girl stood up and went upstairs again. He scuttled out from behind the stove, eased out the back door, and ran to the stable. His wet clothes stuck to him, and the cold made them clammy and dank. Laverty stretched out a hand and took the pastries. "It's blushing like a bride you are," he said, and sank his teeth into one of the pastries.

"I almost got caught. I had to hide behind the stove. I almost got cooked."

"Let that be a lesson to you," Laverty said callously, and chomped away with his eyes rolling.

He finished the pastries while Geordie stood fidgeting, wiped his mouth with the back of one hand, and sighed with satisfaction.

"Laverty?"

"So now you'll be wanting the cat. Well, you'll have it tomorrow."

"Tomorrow?" Geordie asked, vastly disappointed. "Can't I have it today? Where is it?"

"Ah, now, it's in a place and I'll have to get it. Tomorrow when you come home from school it'll be here. Get you gone, now. I have to finish the harness and fix the furnace and take the ashes out, my black curse on 'em. And then take the sleigh downtown for His Worship."

There was nothing for Geordie to do but accept the delay as patiently as he could, so he went back to the house and changed his clothes, wondering by what devious maneuvers Laverty was going to get the cat and why he had hidden behind the stove like a kid. Then he thought of glass eyes for the cat, wrote a letter to order them, and decided to ride downtown with Laverty to mail the letter. It was a delight to ride in the sleigh, warm under the buffalo robe, with the chilly wind in your face and the sleigh bells chiming.

THREE

Geordie's best friend and classmate, Spencer Torrance, who lived in the next house but one to the Suttons, had been kept abreast of developments in the matter of taxidermy, and Geordie told him next morning in school about the cat. Spence had more interest in shooting creatures than in preserving their remains, but he was a good companion and willing to take a hand in anything that was new, so he came home from school with Geordie. They didn't tarry on the way, and when they went into the harness room the cat was lying on the table. They recognized it at once and stared at it in dismay; huge and black, with a white spot surrounding its left eye, it was the dearly beloved pet of Miss Cecily Enders, a redoubtable maiden lady who lived in the next block.

"Good Christmas!" Spence said. "It's Patch! Geordie, do you suppose he shot it?"

Words failed Geordie, for Miss Cecily was a disaster when something aroused her, and nothing in this world could have moved her more than the violent death of Patch. She doted upon Patch, she made a fool of herself over Patch; Patch filled her passionate and frustrated life. Geordie, staring horrified at the corpse, foresaw eventual discovery, Miss Cecily storming into the house like a ranting Fury, and his father (who walked very softly around her for much less than this) casting him into outer darkness. Laverty, that evil man, had betrayed him; he looked at Spence and opened his mouth but no words came out of it.

Spence recovered first. "Let's find Laverty," he said.

They ran out of the harness room into the stable to discover that the two matched grays weren't in their stalls; they ran across the yard and into the kitchen. Ingrid was writing a letter on the table, and looked up with a start when they burst through the door.

"Where's Laverty?" Geordie asked, in a quavering voice. "Ingrid, where's Laverty?"

"He takes your mother to a party. Soon he is back. There is trouble?" She stood up. "Something is not right?" As always, there was a tranquility about her, and it calmed Geordie; the feeling that everything was going along as usual took some of the panic out of him.

"We wanted to see him," he said. "We'll wait in the stable."

They went back to the stable again, and in a short time Laverty drove into the yard. He was rosy from the cold air, and cheerful; there was no hangdog look about him when he saw them, and instead of avoiding their eyes he saluted them with his whip. He pulled the grays up. "Why aren't you after skinnin' him?" he asked. "He's not thawed out, is it?"

Geordie looked at him, caught between a feeling of outrage and a dawning notion that he might have been a fool. "It's Patch!" he burst out finally. "You know it's Patch! How did you—"

"Sure and all it's Patch. Who else would it be? He died yesterday and she wants him stuffed." He began to unhitch the grays, turning his back on them.

"Oh," Geordie said, completely deflated. "Oh." He looked at Spence; Spence looked back at him, and grinned. Soon they were both laughing, and still laughing went into the harness room again.

Patch, as Laverty had suggested, had been frozen and wasn't sufficiently thawed yet to work upon. They moved the table closer to the potbellied stove and stood admiring the departed, turning him once in awhile to hasten his thawing. They heard the horses walking through the stable to their stalls and then Laverty joined them.

"Sure, and he's as big as an elephant," Laverty said, giving the corpse a poke. "It almost broke my back to carry him here."

"How did he get so big?" Spence asked. "He's the biggest cat I ever saw."

"Ah, she had him altered, the wicked creature," Laverty said, "and all the fine spirit in him went into growin'. That and all the calves' liver he ate and the feather cushions he sat on like a lord." Laverty rolled his eyes. "Get your knife, now. It think he's about ready."

Geordie felt the cat, nodded, and went to the house to get his tools. When he returned Laverty had gone off somewhere, and they set to work getting the skin off Patch; they had skinned muskrats and other animals and made a fair job of it. They spread the skin out and trimmed the fat from it, and then were faced with the question of what to do with the tail.

"The book says to skin it out," Spence said, thumbing through the pages.

"We'll never get it sewed up. I think I'll leave the bone in it."

"It'll smell."

"Oh, it'll dry out."

"Huh," Spence said, unconvinced. "Then it says to boil the skull."

"You get his head off," Geordie said. "I'll go get a pan from Ingrid." He went into the kitchen and came back with a small saucepan full of water; they put the cat's head into it and sat it on top of the potbellied stove. This done, they rubbed the recommended chemicals into the skin and tacked it up on the wall to dry. The saucepan began to boil.

"Want to go skating later?" Geordie asked, taking what was left of Patch and depositing it in the garbage can.

In the fullness of time, what with monumental labors, vexations, and compromises, the job was done. It had been a sort of secret enterprise accomplished in the harness room where Geordie's mother and father never came. This was just as well, for the room wasn't improved by the work; an odd and complicated odor now hung in it, and bits of wire, papier-mâché, wax, and whatnot were scattered all about. Laverty had always kept it very neat, but he had given up trying; he couldn't cope with it any longer, and was looking forward to the day when they would be finished and he could straighten up again. Unknown to Geordie he had made an arrangement with Miss Cecily to collect ten dollars when he delivered the finished work, but by the day Geordie stood back and announced that he could do no more Laverty had long since given up that pleasant prospect.

He stood beside the beaming boy, managing not to roar aloud at the creation whose resemblance to the departed Patch was purely coincidental. Patch's aldermanic figure was now more than slender, for the skin hadn't been stretched enough and wasn't well tanned; tanning was a process too complicated for them. His face was very lopsided and held an idiotic grin; he was walleyed, swaybacked, and lumpy, his hair stood up in places, and the untreated tail stuck out sideways at a right angle to his meager body as stiff and straight as a poker. Standing asprawl, as though about to collapse, on a carefully waxed board, he was a horrible parody of the world's most disreputable and underprivileged cat.

"You think she'll like him, Laverty?" Geordie asked proudly, blinded by the joy of creation. "Of course, his tail's a little stiff, but cats carry their tails that way sometimes."

Laverty turned away to gain control of himself, and then turned back. "Ah," he said. "So they do. I've often seen him do it."

Geordie grinned. "I think I'll put a cloth over him and give him an official unveiling when I get there," he said. "Maybe I'll even get her to reimburse me for expenses."

"Ah," Laverty said. "Don't you remember, now? She was to pay ten dollars for the work. I told you and you must have forgot. You were goin' to give me a bit of it for gettin' him and all."

Geordie looked at him and blinked. "I don't think you told me," he said mildly, and took it no further; money was incidental to him at the moment. "I'll go get the

cloth, and take him now."

He went out and returned with a clean pillowcase which he draped over the cat. Then he picked him up. "I'll give you half," he said, as he left.

Bridget, the maid at Miss Cecily's, was an Irish girl and a party to Laverty's maneuvers; when she saw Geordie instead of Laverty bringing Patch home she suspected at once which way the wind was going to blow, and set about trying to temper it. "A good day to you, Mr. Geordie," she said. "Come into the parlor, now, and I'll get Miss Cecily for you. Could I have a bit of a look at him, the poor darlin'?"

"I don't think you'd better," Geordie said. "I want her to see it first."

"Ah, just a bit of a look, Mr. Geordie. It could be a secret between us."

"No," Geordie said. "Go and get her, Bridget."

Bridget saw he was determined, and gave up; she had made her try. She gave him a look that puzzled him and went out, and Geordie glanced about for the best place to stage his triumph. One end of the room was arranged as a "Turkish corner", with several floor lamps of pierced brass, a hookah on an inlaid taboret, beaded curtains at the French doors, a camel saddle, and a vaguely Oriental looking divan smothered under a profusion of draped scarves and pillows, and he decided that would be the place. He took the hookah off the taboret and placed it on the floor, put the covered cat in its place, turned on the lamps, and moved out into the middle of the room.

Presently Miss Cecily swept in, trailing yards of a frilly pink *peignoir* which contrasted oddly with her air of iron virtue. She was very tall and thin, and this was accentuated by an elaborate, high coiffure. She usually carried her jutting patrician nose high and looked down it to outstare everyone, but this afternoon she was almost simpering; she was at once ridiculous and formidable. Ordinarily Geordie would have gone a mile out of his way to avoid her, but today was different.

"Hello, Miss Cecily!" he said, and gave her his slow grin.

"Good afternoon, Geordie," she said. "Bridget tells me that you have brought our dear kitty home."

Her classification of Patch made Geordie stare for a moment, but he recovered quickly. "Yes, Ma'am," he said, and glanced toward the Turkish corner.

"Ah," she said, following his glance, "here he is, the dear one, in the place he loved the most. How clever, how sensitive of you, Geordie, to have guessed it! As he rested among the cushions he was like a great pasha, lordly and indolent but oh! so much the master of all he surveyed and its secrets! Let us look at him now, Geordie. I have been so impatient."

Geordie walked over, whisked off the pillowcase, and turned toward her. She stared; she took a step; her head came forward and there came over her face an expression of incredulity that changed swiftly to a look of outrage and horror. "Oh!" she exclaimed. "Oh, my darling!" Her voice went up and up. "What have they done to you? What have they *done?"* As Geordie stared at her, astounded, her face turned toward him; her eyes glared and her hair, apparently by itself, seemed to spring out like the writhing, snaky locks of Medusa. "Oh, you wicked, wicked boy!" She raised her hands and her fingers bent into claws as though she was going to rush over and take hold of him, and then she suddenly went off into shrieking hysterics.

Geordie had never seen a case of hysterics; the thought that she had suddenly gone out of her mind paralyzed him. He stood rooted, with the uproar washing over him.

Bridget came running in, caught him by the arm, and tugged him toward one of the French doors.

"Get you gone, for the love of Heaven! Get you gone, before she does you a mischief!" she implored, tugging at him. She picked up the cat, thrust it into his arms, and pushed him through the French door. He ran across the lawn as though fiends were after him, hugging the cat, followed by Miss Cecily's shrieks which were suddenly cut off as the door was slammed shut.

By the time Geordie reached home he had recovered enough to decide to take Patch up to his room and conceal him. He managed to do this without being seen, and hid the cat in his closet; after dinner that night he got it out, set it on the desk, and slumped down in the chair to look at it. Now that he had seen someone else's reaction to his work, and such a dramatic reaction at that, he began to see that he had been blinded by his own pride and enthusiasm. As he stared at the cat (and remembered Miss Cecily, a memory that would be with him for years) he began to see how bad it really was, and the longer he looked the worse it got. Finally he turned hot with shame, swung away, and stood up. There was a knock at the door.

"Geordie?" his mother's voice said. "Geordie?"

His first reaction was to hide the cat, but he realized the door was open and she would be able to see any move he made. "Yes, Ma?" he asked.

"May I come in?"

"Yes," he said, and stood waiting.

She came in; her eyes went to the cat, came back to him, and stayed on him. She wasn't going to mention Patch.

"Are you all right, Geordie? You were so quiet at dinner."

"I'm all right, Ma," Geordie said, and then, grateful to her for not pressing him, added: "I'm all right now." He was quiet for a moment. "I stuffed Miss Cecily's cat, and she didn't care for the job. There it is." He turned, and pointed at the perfectly obvious Patch.

She looked at Patch, and managed not to burst out laughing or make a slighting comment.

"I guess it's not very good," he said finally. "When she saw it, it nearly drove her out of her mind. I thought she'd gone crazy. Is she crazy, Ma?"

"She's not as well balanced as she could be, Geordie. She lives all alone, and hadn't anybody to love except Patch. It must be hard to be as lonely as she must be. Lonely people do strange things." She put her arm around him, and looked into his face. "Your first try?"

He nodded.

"Will you want to try some more?"

He nodded again. "I want to, Ma," he said. "With birds, I think. I don't know why I prefer this to law, but I do."

"Does that worry you, Geordie? Do you often think about it?"

"Sometimes," he said, and suddenly didn't feel like talking about it any more. When he really thought about it he wasn't completely sure; things got all mixed up. "I'll do better mounts than Patch."

"Of course you will," she smiled. "Keep him to remind you. Do good ones." She kissed him. "Good night," she said, and went out of the room.

He watched her go, and smiled after her. She had given him great comfort.

FOUR

Toward the end of winter the weather moderated, and the two boys could get out more. The chance of late storms was still too great for the parents of either of them to permit camping trips, so their expeditions were close to home and were daily ones. The country was bleak and cheerless and much of it was still under snow; there was little wildlife in evidence, but the animals left their tracks in the snow. These could be followed, and many of the events in the lives of their makers could be deciphered. The sudden end of a rabbit's wandering trail, a little blood, and the parallel marks of wingtips told them as plainly as though they had seen it that a horned owl had made a successful strike; small footprints and a shallow furrow showed them where a mink had dragged an unlucky muskrat to a place of concealment. They learned a good deal about the territories and routes of animals, and occasionally found the corpse of some creature whose life had been ended by the rigors of winter; following the trails showed them more than they could have found out in the softer seasons, when the vegetation was up and much was concealed.

On week-ends they were usually gone all day on these trips, wandering widely and carrying packs, for they had soon wearied of cold sandwiches and had decided to cook something at noon. Few people not in the last stages of starvation would have enjoyed their cuisine at first, but they improved. Of the two of them, Geordie became the better cook; he had always eaten well at home, and soon got tired of messy lunches. He spent some time with Ingrid, and the results showed it. His cooking wasn't elaborate, for he had no ambitions to be a chef, but it was sound and tasty.

After the ice went out they began to do a little trapping. It was for skins to sell to the fur buyer, not for specimens, for Geordie had lost his taste for stuffing animals after the debacle with Patch and hadn't got it back again. His interest, which had always rather favored birds, slowly swung more toward them as time went on. They had a stronger appeal to his imagination because of their freedom of movement. He read everything about them that he could get his hands on but still he wasn't satisfied. For these books were books of general circulation, somewhat sentimental and not very scientific. He never thought of the University library and its wider selection; if he thought of the University at all it was as a stuffier sort of high school, and it didn't occur to anyone to suggest it to him or to try to clear up his misapprehension.

Besides, he was busy. Having been housebound through the bad weather he had accumulated so much energy that he had to move about. The week-ends were too far apart to be completely satisfying, and as the days began to get longer he and Spence arose early and got out somewhere closer to home, before school. Their muskrat catch along the River north of town, and in the creeks emptying into it, was considerable; they went along without much incident until the morning when they caught the skunk.

Their muskrat traps were set in or near the water, with a wire attached to the trapchain so that the muskrats could dive for deeper water and drown themselves, but this time they knew from seventy yards away that a skunk had blundered into one of them and crawled up the bank, for it had been busily expressing its displeasure and the wind brought the smell to them. They stopped and looked at each other.

"Oh, my," Spence said. "What'll we do now? If we'd brought the rifle we could shoot him, but without it how will we get him out of the trap?"

"Maybe we could leave him until morning, and come back and shoot him then," Geordie said, but as soon as he said it he knew that he couldn't leave the animal in the trap all day and overnight. "We can't come back this afternoon. We've got assembly, and after that it'll be dark."

"Maybe we'd better look at him and see if we can figure something out."

They moved in closer, making faces that expressed distaste, to find that the skunk had moved around enough to beat down the snow; it was in a depression, and out of sight. They had to move closer still; they split up, so that

Spence could move in and peer down into the depression while Geordie made a noise on the other side to distract the victim's attention.

"Hey!" Spence said. "Hey, he's white! He's pure white!"

This was exciting news, for the fur buyer had offered a much higher price for white skunks; the trade prized them, for they were easier to dye or could be used as they were. Geordie forgot his caution, moved in too close, and was lightly sprayed. He fell back and Spence, excited in his turn, also got into the line of fire. They both were momentarily dismayed, but now that the damage was done and the prospect of riches was before them they had to go through with the enterprise.

"We got to get him," Spence said. "If we leave him, a hawk or a horned owl will eat him. We got to get him, Geordie."

"How?"

"With a long stick. Hit him on the head."

They separated and ran excitedly about, and then came back and began to belabor the skunk. This didn't seem to work very well; the unfortunate center of their attentions ran around at the end of the trapchain and desperately filled the air with its scent, a good deal of which ended up on their clothing. They were too excited to have thoughts of the cruelty of their method and were so inured to the smell by this time that they didn't notice it any longer; they moved closer to the doomed animal, took what it had to give, and finally did it in. They stood above it, winded, smelling to heaven, and triumphant, and then Geordie stooped and took it out of the trap. He put it into the bag that they carried with them, and they grinned happily at each other.

"Man, he was something. Maybe if we'd just teased him long enough he'd have run out of juice."

"It might have taken a long time," Spence said, and was suddenly struck with a thought. "You guess it's time for school?"

"School?" Geordie asked. "Good Heavens!" He looked at the sun. "We're late. Let's go."

Forgetting to set the trap again, they began to run. They ran and trotted most of the way to school, dangling the bag, stumbling and puffing; there were no students outside. Geordie hid the bag beneath one of the bushes in the yard, and they went into the building, along the corridor, and into their room.

The boys and girls were at their desks and there was a substitute teacher at the front, a man; they hadn't seen him before and their first swift impression of him was an unfavorable one. He was tall and thin, with a pale, thin face and a thin, pursed mouth; he stared at them with disapproval, but before he could speak the pupils nearest to Geordie and Spence clutched their noses and began to make extravagant gestures, and in the twinkling of an eye the class was in an uproar.

The teacher pounded on the desk to no avail, and then moved swiftly down the aisle; he looked as though he was going to take hold of them, but when he got near them he recoiled. His pale face turned scarlet, and he raised a lanky arm. "Out!" he said. "Out in the hall. Go!"

They went out, and he followed them. Standing over them, still scarlet and gasping for breath, he waved a hand around. "The idea! Disrupting the class with this . . . this mephitic stench, this horrible . . . Coming into my class in this . . . Young ruffians!" He stretched out a long arm for Geordie, and quickly withdrew it again. "Ruffian!" Further words failed him, and he stood shifting from one foot to the other, opening and closing his mouth.

Geordie had never been called a ruffian, and the strange gyrations of the teacher, without dignity or, so far as he could see, reason, were too much for him. "Yes, sir," he said. "Go to Hell."

The teacher froze, and stared at him; his color grew even higher. His eyes glared; his hands came up and he took a step forward, but once more the aura of skunk drove him back. "Insolence!" he exclaimed. "Obscene insolence as well! To the office! Come to the office at once!"

He took a wide half circle around them and started for the office in a rush. The two boys, confused and a little frightened now, looked at each other and followed him. He whisked through the anteroom and slammed the door, and they could hear his raised voice as he talked to the Principal. Presently he came out again, walked past them without a look, and vanished. Mr. Moore, the Principal, put his head out the door, looked mildly from one of them to the other, flinched, and said: "Meet me outside."

They went out and waited by the door, quiet and subdued, for Mr. Moore, the fountainhead of all authority, was an unknown quantity, mysterious and remote. He joined them, and got upwind. Rather chubby, calm and unruffled, he stood and looked at them for a moment; they could make nothing from his expression. "Now, then," he said finally. "How did you get so fragrant?"

"Sir?" Geordie asked, stalling.

"The smell," he said. "Did you put it on yourselves?"

"No, sir. We were trapping, and we caught a skunk."

"It's really strong, you know."

"Yes, sir," Spence said. "We were late, and so we came directly to class."

"I see. And then you told Mr. Jenks to go to Hell."

"Yes, sir," Geordie said. He looked down, twisted his toe into the ground, and looked up again. "He called us ruffians. We didn't *do* anything, Mr. Moore. We were late, that was all. We weren't behaving like ruffians."

"He's a city man," Mr. Moore said. "Perhaps he was overexcited. It's his first day here. Your teacher's been taken sick."

Geordie felt certain that Mr. Moore knew that their regular teacher would have acted differently.

"Well," Mr. Moore said. "I think you had better get home and clean yourselves up. Don't come back today. I'll have to talk to your fathers and see what we'll do. Off you go, now."

"Yes, sir," they said in chorus. "Thank you, Mr. Moore."

He waved at them, and they turned away. They collected the bag, and on the way home they agreed that Mr. Moore had been very reasonable, although they wished that he had seen fit to fix matters without bringing their fathers into it; neither of them looked forward to the unpleasant conferences that were sure to ensue.

"I guess," Spence said finally, "we do smell pretty bad. Do you think they're going to act the same way at home that everybody did at school?"

"We can go to our stable and get Laverty to bury our clothes, and wash before we go in the house. People are always talking about burying their clothes when a skunk gets them. Laverty can get us some clean clothes from the house."

"What'll we do about the skunk?"

"We'd better skin him now," Geordie said. "We can tack his hide up on the outside of the barn. Around at the back."

They started to skin the skunk beside the street, but an unknown lady of patrician appearance came along in a gleaming electric brougham and stopped to watch them. Under her amazed regard they grew uneasy, and decided to finish the operation behind the stable.

Although Laverty had done his best, Geordie was still faintly redolent from his adventure when his father came in. His mother wasn't home; she had gone with a friend that day to the Amana Colonies twenty-five miles or so away and hadn't returned yet. She had wanted to buy a chair and the Germans at Amana, quiet, friendly people from Hesse who lived in a communal fashion, were such fine craftsmen that she visited them whenever she was looking for furniture. After finding out from Ingrid where his wife was, Alfred Sutton reluctantly decided not to wait for her. He called up the stairs, and Geordie came slowly down and found him in the living room. He was standing by a window, and obviously didn't relish the situation. To Geordie, quite conscious of sin but not really understanding all the uproar that had resulted from the simple trapping of a skunk, he seemed as always a little remote, a man of a different world from Geordie's where he had a mysterious power and everyone's respect.

"Hi, Dad," Geordie said.

"Hello, Geordie. Shall we sit down? I've had a talk with Mr. Moore."

"Yes, sir," Geordie said, and sat down on the davenport.

His father sat down next to him, raised his eyebrows almost imperceptibly, and moved a little further away. "Your teacher," he said, "will be ill for some time, and Mr. Jenks will probably finish out the term. In view of what has happened, I do not think that it would be to your advantage to remain in his class. I have made arrangements for you to finish the term at Prairie View

Academy. You will not be punished."

"Yes, sir," Geordie said, thinking again of his father's power. Everything had been done; smoothly and invisibly there had been conferences with Mr. Moore and the head of Prairie View, punishment had been averted, and his life had been changed. "Yes, sir," he said again. "Will Spence go there too, Dad?"

"Yes," his father said. "I'm sure you will both do well there. Both Spence's father and I think that public school is best, but . . . From what I understand, you were justified in objecting to Mr. Jenks' treatment of you, but you were not justified in cursing him. There are other ways to object. One doesn't lose one's temper with a fool."

"Yes, sir. But, Dad, we were so surprised. He acted as though we had done it on purpose, he didn't give us time to explain. He called us ruffians, and I guess I got mad."

"I said that I thought you were justified, but that I wished you had used other means. I hope that you will recall this next time a situation of this sort develops."

"Yes, sir. I'll try."

"I hope so," Alfred Sutton said. He was silent for a moment, looking at the floor. Geordie sat quietly, wishing that he could go. Presently his father looked up. "You are almost college age, Geordie," he said. "You'll be going to college in the fall. Do you think now that the business with the polecat might have been a little juvenile?"

Geordie's heart sank, but he tried to explain. "He was white, Dad," he said. "They're worth a lot more when they're white, and we wanted to get him before an owl or something else did."

"Ah, yes," Alfred Sutton said, and although he tried to get interest into his voice Geordie knew it wasn't there.

He went on. "Your courses the first year will be general, but it's not at all too early to begin to think what you want to be. Have you ever considered the Army? Old Geordie was a soldier, you know."

"I know," Geordie said.

"You might consider West Point, or Annapolis," his father said. "They lead to good, professional careers, and I think I could manage an appointment." He stood up. "Think about them, Geordie," he said, and smiled. "I'll let you go now. Dinner will probably be a little late, with your mother at Amana, and you must have some studying to do. You will start at Prairie View tomorrow."

"Yes, sir," Geordie said, and left the room. As he climbed the stairs his depression deepened, for his father had been so measured and just about school and so obviously not interested at all in the skunk or anything that pertained to it. His tone when he had said "Ah, yes" had stopped anything that he, Geordie, had wanted to say.

FIVE

The two boys, after being more or less isolated as aliens for a time at Prairie View Academy, were finally accepted by their companions just as signs of spring began to appear in the land. The snow disappeared and the thawing earth turned dark and muddy; roads became quagmires for a time. The River rose in its season and dropped again, a thin frost of green stole across the world and burgeoned; the blue pasqueflowers, much like crocuses, starred the prairie where it had not been broken and changed by the plow and were followed by a tide of other blossoms. Birds that had wintered in the south began to appear in increasing numbers, some to journey further north and some to stay, and their voices took the place of the winter wind's. The dark and bitter season was over and in reluctant retreat.

After the roads became passable again and it was possible to move about freely, Geordie and Spence greased their traps, hung them up, divided the money they had made, and resumed their week-end expeditions. They were intoxicated by the return of life all about them and the warming air, the sunrises and sunsets over the vast reach of the prairies, and their freedom. They could camp overnight again, and looked forward to longer camps after school was out.

About the middle of April someone gave the city library a bird book that had an extended treatment of the Wilson's phalarope in it and the librarian, knowing of Geordie's interest, recommended it to him. He had seen phalaropes the previous year and found a nest or two, for a few of them nested in the vicinity, but he hadn't known very much about them. He had been unaware that the birds migrated to South America and that it was the male which made the nest and brooded the eggs, and that it was the female (or sometimes several of them) which pursued the male in the mating season. This was so unusual, being a reversal of the actions of other birds that he knew, that he was fascinated by it. The fact that the phalarope flew all the way to and from South America, through Central America and Mexico and the Mississippi Valley, was fascinating too; it seemed like such a small bird for all that flying, through jungles and mountains. It was the first bird about which he had been able to gather such complete information; it was a wonderful creature, and after learning so much about it he had to have one.

Ordinarily the two boys spent a good deal of time

along the River, or near it, for Geordie's father had bought him a rowboat the year before and they liked getting about in it; now they began to haunt the prairie sloughs, for the phalarope was a bird of the marshy meadows and could be expected to appear in them. The sloughs, oases of moisture in the dry, grassy prairies, contained a great number of birds; ducks nested near them, and there were always terns, blackbirds, coots, killdeers, and many other species gathered around them or in the air over them. Life was more concentrated about them than along the River, and there was always something to see. After exploring a number of them they finally picked one with a shallow pond covering six or seven acres in the middle of it, and pitched their tent among a few straggly trees on a rise that stood a few feet above the plain. The trees were swamp oaks five or six feet high and how they had got there was a mystery, for they were the only trees in all the wide view.

Someone must have planted them there and at first the boys thought that they had discovered a burial mound, for they had heard about the Mound Builders who had lived in Iowa before the Indians appeared. They didn't know that Mound Builders had always lived along the rivers and creeks, and the boys dug around with great enthusiasm in a search for artifacts. They didn't find any, because there were none, but for a long time afterward they liked to think that somewhere deep below their tent were mouldering bones and a little pottery placed there long ago by a vanishing race.

It was a little too early for the phalaropes when they first set up their camp, but the killdeers were there and they shot two of them with Spence's .22 rifle for Geordie to practice stuffing. The bullets didn't leave too much of the birds, but enough. The shotgun would have been better, but it is a noisy weapon, and they only wanted to use it once, to get a phalarope, lest there should be someone around who would hear it and make trouble for them. They also had slingshots, and they collected several blackbirds. Blackbirds were so commonplace as to be expendable and killing several of them didn't produce the same feeling of lawbreaking and sin as the killing of a more delicate and rarer bird.

They took the shotgun to the tent, each of them carrying half of it under his clothes, and hid it, wrapped up in greasy rags and oilcloth to protect it from the weather. They visited the blind every weekend, and then on a bright Sunday morning Spence stuck his head out of the tent just as three phalaropes flew past. They were females, close enough for him to see the cinnamon neck-stripe that males do not have.

"They're here!" he announced, pulling his head back inside and turning around. "Three of them just went by." Out went his head again; Geordie jumped out of his blankets and joined him.

Spence pointed; the three birds, flying together, swung a wide, fast circle and landed at the pond's edge, waded out until they were waterborne, and began to spin about to stir up the small organisms they fed upon. It was a characteristic phalarope gesture.

Geordie got the old binoculars and watched the birds, fascinated. They were pretty things, with their longish necks and bills and smooth feathers; that they had started to feed so quickly indicated that they had just come in from a long and mysterious journey. He had seen phalaropes many times before, but then they had been just birds to him; now they were the focus of an interest that had suddenly strengthened, for the book had revealed their uniqueness and by so doing had suggested how much there was to know of all other birds as well. He was so engrossed in watching them that Spence finally grew impatient and withdrew into the tent.

By now the phalaropes had finished their feeding and

returned to the shore, where they stood together at the edge of the water. Spence returned fully dressed and with the gun. They took it out of its wrappings and loaded it. The birds were well out of range, and they decided to see if they could walk up close enough to them for a shot. Geordie had the gun, and handed it to Spence.

"You shoot one," he said.

"You're a better shot than I am."

"I'd rather you did it," Geordie said. "I feel queasy about it now."

Spence stared at him. "You mean you're going to quit shooting?" he asked.

"I'm not going to quit shooting. It's just these particular birds."

Spence shook his head; this was all too much for him. He took the gun, and they walked around the edge of the pond. The birds flushed when they were still too far away for a shot, crossed the pond, and landed again.

"We'll never get close enough to them this way," Geordie said. "Why don't you stay here and crouch down, and I'll walk around."

Spence nodded, and Geordie went on. He got quite close to them this time before they flushed, uttering low, nasal, grunting sounds; they flew back across the pond again. He saw Spence rise when they neared him and fire; one of them went down, and he watched this with an emotion that was a strange mixture of regret and pleasure. He now had one to mount. When he reached Spence again, Spence handed him the bird. It wasn't quite dead; lying in his hand, beyond the effort of fluttering, it looked at him with dark and luminous eyes, gave a feeble shudder, and died. He stroked it and for a moment almost wept for this dainty far traveler so wilfully deprived of life. Then he went to the tent for bits of cotton to plug the shot wounds so that the feathers wouldn't be stained with blood. He was still in his pajamas.

The rest of that spring passed pleasantly and the summer, after school was out, was fine and free. The two boys weren't home a great deal; they spent most of their time camping in the marshes or along the River, and made a long float trip downstream, camping where the spirit moved them and stopping for as long as they pleased. They came back by train, with the boat in the baggage car, sunburned, scratched by briars and well bitten by the insects of the season, esteeming themselves as hardy adventurers and ready for some home cooking after a diet of mulligan stew and fish.

They had climbed river bluffs amid the ferns and wild grape and wandered over prairie not yet changed, with its golden coreopsis, white and purple prairie clover, yellow toadflax, and crepe-petalled primrose; they had made fine camps under the riverside trees and had plenty of time to watch the birds and animals about them. Their progress had been like that of the prairie rivers, wandering and slow; a sudden and violent summer hailstorm and several thundershowers had been the only thing to disturb their leisurely way. They spent much time swimming and jumped off all the bridges they came to, and the few people they met talked to them as though they were mature men on a sensible outing. Their memories were of golden dawns, warm, lively days, and long, quiet sunsets when feeding fish dimpled the water, owls awoke, and the creatures of the night began to stir beyond the firelight to go about their concerns.

One day they had an experience that they often

laughed about later, a thing that happened the day after they got back. It was very hot that day, and not feeling energetic enough to go very far they went swimming close to town with a few of their friends. They were all naked; standing on the shore to recover their breath after a tussle in the water, they were startled to hear a girl's voice calling: "Hoohoo!" They turned, to see a neighbor's twelve-year-old who had somehow wandered down to the river. They desperately tried to cover themselves with their hands, and before they collected themselves sufficiently to take refuge in the water heard her say: "Geordie Sutton, your hair's all wet. You'll sure catch it when you get home!"

SIX

Holding the phalarope, lost in recollection of the spring and summer that were gone, Geordie was recalled to the dim room by his mother's voice calling him from downstairs. He started violently and almost dropped the bird; he had been so completely immersed in his reverie that for a moment he didn't know where he was, and looked wildly around in an effort to identify his surroundings. His mother called again; this time there was a questioning note in her voice. This settled him down and the room became familiar again, familiar and solid and reassuring. He walked to the door and called back to her. "I'll be right down, Ma. I'm sorry."

He walked back to the desk and set the phalarope down in its accustomed place and suddenly, when his hand was empty of it, he began to cry. The flood of memories of the happy, carefree summer and the confusion and uncertainty about the future were too much for him. His hands grasped the edges of the desk and he rocked back and forth fighting against the tears.

Before he managed to get himself under control again there was a knock at the door. He dried his eyes, took a deep breath, and said: "Come in."

The door opened and Uncle Harry, Lavinia Sutton's brother, entered. He was a big, ruddy man, a dealer in grain and a duck hunter, a bachelor who often went to Chicago and the east and was therefore considered quite cosmopolitan. He was amused by this, and would infrequently drop hints about gay eastern girls to sustain it. The gay girls never saw him; he had a quiet arrangement in the town that suited him, and he spent his spare time away from shooting or business with several professors at the University or reading books of foreign travel. He was a quietly observant, sensitive fellow, fond of Geordie, and saw at once that Geordie was upset. "Hello, old boy," he said.

"Hi, Uncle Harry. I was just about to—"

"Don't hurry," Uncle Harry said. "I'll tell them to start eating, that you'll soon be down. I just thought that you might want to go to a lecture with me at the University this evening. Came up to ask you."

Geordie was grateful for this circumlocution and wanted to express his appreciation by accepting, but he was a bit dubious; he still felt shaken, and he thought of college lectures as stuffy. "Well . . ." he said.

"You'd be interested in it," Uncle Harry said. "It's about an island called Laysan, off in the Pacific somewhere. Has a lot of rare birds and things on it. Satterthwaite, the Biology man, was there last year and took some pictures he's going to show with the magic lantern."

"In the Pacific?" Geordie asked.

"Out near Hawaii. Volcanic island, I think."

Geordie looked at him, unconsciously nodding his head, for suddenly, in his mind's eye, he saw a lovely misty dark cone arising from the sea, hiding secret things that were new and strange. "A volcano?" he asked.

"I doubt it's a volcano now," Uncle Harry went on. "I think this is the top of an old one, just above the water. A nesting island for millions of birds. You'd better come."

"All right," Geordie said.

"Good. Wash your face and hands and come down when you're ready." He grinned and went out of the room.

Geordie stood for a moment smiling at the closed door. The emotional upheaval of a few minutes past had retreated into the back of his mind.

They moved into the living room after dessert, for Geordie's father liked to have a demitasse there, and as they sat about waiting to go to the lecture Uncle Harry told them a little about Dr. Satterthwaite, whom he called "Sat."

"Dr. Conover was at the University before Sat and did a great deal for the Museum collection. Sat's carried his work on awfully well. It's a very good university museum, and from what little Sat's said about his ideas for the future I gather that he has some that will make other museum people sit up and take notice. This Laysan Island he's talking about tonight is way off in the Pacific, out of the shipping lanes and deserted most of the time.

It's famous among biologists all over the world for the

hundreds of thousands of sea birds that nest on it."

"It sounds very exotic," Geordie's mother said. "Why don't we all go? Wouldn't you like to hear him, Alfred?"

"I'd better stay here," Geordie's father said. "There's a brief or two I should look over, but the rest of you go along. Harry can drive the car. Geordie, go out to the stable and ask Laverty to bring it around."

Geordie nodded and went out to the stable and routed out Laverty, who came downstairs in his undershirt, muttering under his breath while he lit the big brass gas headlights, the oil tail light, and cranked the engine. They drove out under the porte-cochere; Laverty went back to the stable, and Geordie ran into the house to get his mother and Uncle Harry.

They started for the campus, which was near the river; before they reached it the quiet of the night was shattered by gongs and the clatter of galloping horses, and they pulled over and stopped to let a fire engine go by. The steam pumper was belching sparks, the driver leaned forward like a racer to hold his great plunging gray horses, and the whole splendid affair seemed to shake the earth as it roared past them and skidded around a corner further down the street. Geordie was still tingling with the excitement of it when they reached MacBride Hall, where the auditorium was, and parked the car.

"Let's hurry a little," Uncle Harry said, as they all got out of the car. "Maybe we can have a word with Sat before he begins. You know him, Geordie, I'm sure."

"No, sir," Geordie said.

"What? Hasn't your father . . . ?" He turned to his sister. "How's this, Vin? Haven't you or Alfred . . . ? I mean, with his interests, it seems very odd that he hasn't been at the house."

"Yes," Geordie's mother said. "Let's not go into it now, Harry."

"H'm. Well, all right. We'll try to fix it." He picked up the pace and they reached the auditorium and went in. The big room had a rather dusty, formal air and there were a number of people sitting in the seats, talking and waiting for the show to begin. In the center aisle, where the projector sat on a table, there was a lean, bald man talking to the projectionist, who gazed sadly at him and nodded occasionally. The lean man made quite a few gestures and talked rapidly, in little bursts; he seemed an intense fellow, and stabbed a finger at the other now and then to emphasize a point but grinned when he did it. A sort of lively good nature seemed to emanate from him despite his intensity, and Geordie felt drawn to him.

Uncle Harry marched up to him and laid a hand on his shoulder, and he turned around. He looked at Uncle Harry blankly for an instant, still thinking about what he had been saying to the projectionist, and then smiled broadly. "Hello, Harry. Good evening, Mrs. Sutton. Glad you could come. New territory for you, isn't it?"

"It is for Mrs. Sutton and Geordie, my nephew. You'll probably have to cope with him presently. We'd like to see you for a moment after the show, if you haven't anything better to do."

"Nothing to do. At least, nothing better." He shook hands with Geordie. "Seems to me I've heard about you from your uncle. Duck hunter, aren't you?" He stabbed the finger. "Know the marshes, h'm? You're just the man I've been looking for."

"Yes, sir," Geordie said, a little confused to have the finger stabbed at him and to be noticed so pleasantly. People of his father's generation were usually polite and a little distant, as though they were thinking of something else; the professor made him feel that he had quickly been accepted as an equal.

"We'll see you later, then," Uncle Harry said, and moved them both before him into seats.

Geordie sat down in a pleasant glow; as his mother and uncle began to talk together he fell to wondering why the professor, a learned man who had been all over the world, should be looking for a duck hunter who knew the marshes and for himself in particular. Although he had often moved about the campus he didn't know very much about the place; it had always seemed as remote from him as the City Hall or the Capitol in Washington.

Satterthwaite left the projectionist and walked up onto the stage. The audience grew quiet, and Satterthwaite clasped his hands in front of him and began to speak rather formally.

"My talk tonight," he began, "is about an island called Laysan, the summit of an old volcanic peak near the northern end of the Hawaiian Islands chain. This island became famous before the turn of the century for its remarkable nesting colonies of oceanic birds, which must have numbered a million, and for five other species that are unique to Laysan: a teal, a rail, a miller bird, a honey eater, and a finch. These species are unique because they evolved in an isolated environment.

"Dr. Conover, my predecessor here who many of you remember, and whom we have to thank for many specimens in our museum collection, went to Laysan nine years ago with an expedition from our University. He took a number of pictures, and an ornithologist with the party, Dr. Blandford, wrote an outstanding paper on the bird life. I am familiar with the pictures and the paper; ever since my first acquaintance with them I have longed to go to Laysan, and last year I had the opportunity."

He paused and grinned, as though he was pleased to have got through the introduction. He seemed to relax all at once; he unclasped his hands and stuck them into his pockets and took a few short steps back and forth. "It was a wonderful trip," he said, "and I'm glad I went when I did, for some very bad things are happening on the island.

"It was once remote and undisturbed, but around 1890 it was leased for twenty years to a guano company by the kingdom of Hawaii. The company manager was a German captain named Schlemmer, and around 1903 he introduced rabbits on Laysan to add to his food supply, for it was expensive to import provisions and fresh meat was hard to get. Maybe he had some idea of selling rabbit meat to the ships that came for the guano. At any rate, the rabbits began to increase, and having no natural enemies on the island they kept on increasing. By the time that Dr. Conover was there, nine years later, there were indications that they were destroying the vegetation, outrunning their food supply. When I was there last year this destruction had progressed, and a good deal of the vegetation that had once covered the island and stabilized the sand had been eaten. The petrels and shearwaters, which nested in burrows, were in many cases smothered when sand shifted over the burrow entrances in storms or high winds. In addition, many of the sailors from the guano ships had talked in various ports about the immense numbers of birds, and this brought feather-hunters, Japanese mostly, who killed hundreds of thousands of birds for their feathers, which they sold to the millinery trade.

"Of the two things, I think the well-intentioned introduction of the rabbits was the worst. It is a classic example of what happens when nature is interfered with, for an ecological balance that worked was destroyed. The feather-hunters were finally controlled when President Roosevelt, upon being told of their depredations, set aside the chain of islands as a wildlife refuge, but nothing has been done about the rabbits. They have continued to increase. The guano operation ceased in 1904, the last Japanese feather raid took place in 1909, but the rabbits are still there.

"That is a short history of what has happened on Laysan Island. Now we can have the pictures."

Several hands went up, but the lights began to go out and the hands went down again. "I will answer questions later," Dr. Satterthwaite said, and moved to the side of the screen.

The first picture appeared. It had been taken from the sea, and showed a flattish island beyond the surf, a shining beach beyond which low herbage could be seen, and a great number of birds in the air.

Geordie was a little disappointed to see the flatness of Laysan, for he had clung to a volcano in his mind, but as the pictures went on to show the house, sheds, and the tall tower that had all been built by the guano company, and then to show several palm trees, and then vast, almost unbelievable colonies of albatrosses, shearwaters, boobies, man-of-war birds and teal, little flightless rails, seals and huge turtles on the beach, he grew more and more fascinated. Satterthwaite kept up a running comment on the pictures, explaining them, and between his words and the pictures themselves a little world was built up, a remote, wonderful world full of strange birds and beasts that were extraordinarily tame because few of them had known men, a world of beautiful lonely beaches, lovely warm days, and sometimes wild storms. Geordie thought of camping on such a place and having it all to himself like Robinson Crusoe, of fishing to his heart's content, and watching the endless play of life about him.

He had never seen so many birds; he hadn't thought there were that many in the world. Satterthwaite had pictures of their strange courtship antics, their nests, and their habits; the pretty little honey eaters singing from the bushes, the finches perching on the shoulders of the expedition members, and great turtles turned over to be butchered for food. There were pictures of men collecting eggs, men swimming, fishing or working on bird skins, men walking through thousands of nesting seabirds that seemed to pay no attention to them at all. When the show ended and the lights came on Geordie felt lost for a long moment; he had been so completely on the island that it was a great wrench to be brought back to the auditorium again.

Applause rippled around the auditorium, and he turned to see his mother and his uncle both smiling at him. As people began to get up to leave, a few of them gathered around Satterthwaite, who had come down from the stage. Uncle Harry got up and made his way to Satterthwaite too. They got their heads together for a moment, and a short, dark man came and joined them. The man and Uncle Harry moved off a step or two, and stood waiting. Presently all the people around Satterthwaite were answered, and the last one turned away. Then he, Uncle Harry and the dark man drew together and walked over to where Geordie and his mother were waiting.

"You liked Laysan, I hear," Satterthwaite said to Geordie.

"Yes, sir. I think it's wonderful. I'd love to go there."

"Well, we'll do the best we can at the moment. This is Dr. Black, the Director of our Museum, and he has something to show you."

Geordie shook hands with Dr. Black, who had a slight cast in one eye that gave him a faintly sinister air, or would have at any other time. "Yes," Dr. Black said.

"We would like to show you something. We'll go upstairs to the Museum, if you don't mind."

They went into the hall where Dr. Black turned on a few upstairs lights, climbed the staircase to the third floor, and followed Dr. Black and Satterthwaite into the Bird Hall. Their footsteps echoed hollowly in the empty hall; the cases glittered in the dim light. It was somewhat ghostly and strange; the shadowy cases were full of birds half seen, and Geordie wondered why he had never been in the Museum before. It was rather extraordinary that he had never made the effort to come here, but it was understandable; his father had never mentioned it, his mother hadn't thought of it, and his teacher at school hadn't been interested in natural history. The dim, tantalizing glimpses of all the birds as he walked along, added to the excitement that had been aroused in him by the lecture.

Dr. Black came to a door and unlocked it and turned on a dim light; they followed him around a semi-circular wall and through another door, and he turned on more lights. Geordie caught his breath, for he seemed to be standing under an open sky with scattered white clouds in it, on a sandy place, surrounded by real bushes and nesting and flying birds that he had seen on the screen a short while before during the lecture. All around, beyond the distant beach, was the sea, shading off into lovely colors and gleaming close to the shore with the whiteness of breaking waves. He was on Laysan; the illusion was perfect to his startled eyes.

"This cyclorama, this new departure in museum exhibits," Dr. Black said, "is entirely Dr. Satterthwaite's idea, quite original with him. We think it's wonderful."

"Really superb!" Uncle Harry said, and turning impulsively took Satterthwaite's hand and pumped it up and down."Sat, it's marvelous. It will revolutionize museums everywhere. I congratulate you, I really do."

Satterthwaite tried to look modest. "Thanks, Harry. You're the first outsiders to see it. Don't say anything to anybody. We want to surprise people with it. We'll put a glass front on, and people can stand there and think they're on the Island."

He went on talking, grinning with pride in his—and Dr. Black's—accomplishment, but Geordie had stopped listening to him and was engrossed in the surrounding details; the beautifully mounted flying birds suspended by thin wires, the perspective so skilfully done that it was difficult to tell where the actual objects left off and the painted background began, the rocks and bushes and different species of birds. There were even rabbits, which Dr. Satterthwaite had said were destroying the vegetation. Looking at all this and utterly fascinated with it, Geordie suddenly thought of his phalarope and instantly knew why he had stuffed it, blundering attempt though it was. This was what he wanted to do, this was the answer suddenly revealed, and he had a moment of giddiness to find it at last plainly before him. His place was going to be somewhere in the scheme of things that could bring such a wonderful group about.

A hand fell on his shoulder and he looked up, startled. Satterthwaite was standing beside him. "How do you like it, my boy?" he asked.

"It's the most wonderful thing I've ever seen!" Geordie burst out.

"Perhaps you have the vocation, h'm?" Satterthwaite nodded. "You take a course with me, I think, and Dr. Black starts a course in museum techniques this coming semester. Between us we can soon find out, and so can you. It's a rewarding life, even if there's not much money in it." He grinned, and the finger shot out. "The duck shooting season starts soon. Why don't we do some shooting together? Call me up, and we can plan something."

"Yes, sir!" Geordie said with delight. "I certainly will. Thank you very much."

Uncle Harry joined them. "Our friends have been very kind," he said, "and now we'd better let them go. Thank Dr. Black, Geordie."

Geordie went to thank Dr. Black, and soon they were all walking down the staircase. The three men were ahead; Geordie walked with his mother, almost like a somnambulist. She had seen his reaction to the cyclorama and heard what he and Satterthwaite had said to each other, and was disturbed that she had done nothing to give him the opportunity to know of such things sooner; all she had done had been to intercede between the boy and his father's impatience, and that hadn't been very much. She felt at the moment that she had failed her son, and hoped that she could make this failure up somehow. "Geordie," she said, "I'm sorry that I haven't done more to help you."

He turned and smiled at her; there was a sweetness in his smile that twisted her heart. "If you hadn't asked Uncle Harry to dinner we wouldn't be here," he said.

She nodded and smiled back at him. It was good of him to say that she had helped by asking Harry to dinner, but she wished he hadn't said it. It was the sort of thing that harassed men say to women when the women have done something that required no real planning or forethought.

SEVEN

"I have an inclination," Uncle Harry said, when they reached the car, "to treat everybody to ice cream."

"That would be nice," Lavinia Sutton said. "The sea air gave me an appetite."

Uncle Harry cranked the car and drove them downtown to the city's best bakery store, which had a room furnished with marble-topped tables and iron chairs. There he ordered ice cream and macaroons. The ice cream was famous for miles around, for the baker made it himself in a big freezer. Little was said until they had eaten half of their portions.

"I saw that bird on your desk when I was in your room this evening, Geordie," Uncle Harry said finally. "Where did you get it?"

"I stuffed it. Spence and I shot it in the spring."

"It looked very good," Uncle Harry said. "I didn't know you were a taxidermist. What sort of bird is it?"

"It's a Wilson's phalarope," Geordie said. "I found a book in the library about it. The male sits on the eggs."

"Poor fellow. But that's not the first bird you've stuffed, is it?"

"No, sir. I practiced on some others so I'd know what to do when I got the phalarope."

"I see," Uncle Harry said, and indeed he was able to understand a good deal. "How long has this been going on?"

"Since last winter, I guess. I read about the phalarope then, and after that I wanted one."

Geordie bent to finish the last of his ice cream, and Uncle Harry exchanged a look with his sister. It was a questioning look, as though to inquire whether she had known how long and steadfastly Geordie had held to his desire; she answered it with a slight negative shake of her head, and said: "I . . . we didn't really know, Harry."

"Well," Uncle Harry said, "we do now." He turned to Geordie. "I'm going to ask them to send you a card for the museum library," he said. "They've got much better books for your purpose, and you won't have to wait until college opens to begin reading them."

"That's something I'd appreciate very much."

Uncle Harry signaled for his check, paid it, and they went out and drove home. Alfred Sutton was still in the living room, with a card table in front of him covered with papers; he pushed it away and stood up. "Was it a good lecture, Geordie?" he asked.

"Yes, sir. It was about the best I ever heard. You

should have come, Dad. I wished you were there." He looked at his Uncle Harry, for they had promised not to tell about the cyclorama.

"Sat showed us a remarkable thing he's done," Uncle Harry said, "but we said we wouldn't mention it. You'll be able to see it soon, anyhow."

"I'll wait," Alfred Sutton said. "You'd better get to bed, now, Geordie."

"All right," Geordie said, and turned away. He stopped at the door. "Thank you an awful lot, Uncle Harry. I . . . For taking me, and for the card." He went out of the room, and they heard him climbing the stairs.

"The card?" Alfred Sutton asked.

"A card for the museum library. I'll get him one. It's a good three weeks before the term begins. Might as well give him a head start. I think it's rather remarkable that he was so steady in that business about his phalarope. He hasn't had much encouragement, you know."

"I know," Alfred Sutton said. "What was this about the phalarope?"

Uncle Harry told him; he listened closely, but with no change of expression. "It looks to me," Uncle Harry went on, "as though he has a very real inclination, Alfred, and that you've been too busy to notice it."

"It is difficult to know what a boy is doing or thinking most of the time," Alfred Sutton said. "The poet was quite right when he wrote that a boy's will is the wind's will."

He glanced at his wife, but she wasn't looking at him. Her head was bent, her glance was on the floor; she knew her husband's hopes and intentions for Geordie and suspected that her brother guessed them too now and was trying to plead Geordie's case in the only way he could. She couldn't be disloyal to her husband even though she disagreed with him, and at the same time she couldn't be disloyal to Geordie and the future he seemed to be finding for himself. She was in a nerve-racking predicament, and as the two men fenced with each other she felt that an iron band was inexorably tightening around her head and would soon crush it. She would have to leave, she couldn't listen to any more. "I think I had better go to bed," she said, looking up with the best smile she could manage. "Thank you, Harry, for the nice evening. Come again as soon as you can."

She left the room, and the two men watched her go.

"I suppose I should be going too," Uncle Harry said, deciding that he had said enough for the moment.

"Why not stay long enough for a game?" Alfred Sutton asked. "After we've finished you can take the car, bring it back in the morning, and we'll drop you on the way downtown."

"Well, all right. I'll get the board and the chessmen out while you gather your papers together. I really don't feel like going to bed quite yet."

After Geordie had gotten to his room and closed the door he felt his way to the desk, turned on the student's lamp, and sat down. He was suddenly very tired from all the events of the day and the emotional impact of those events upon him. The revelation of the way he wanted to spend his life, now that he was alone and undisturbed, completely occupied his mind; it made him a little light-headed, and filled him with an odd, rather disembodied sense of joy. He thought of the books he would be able to read when the card came, of the library that would lead him into the world he was so eager to enter, of being able to see the actual mechanics of museum work and possibly participate in them. Above all this, mistily superimposed upon it, were thoughts of expeditions to places wondrous and strange. In his exalted state he was like a newly-made knight at his vigil before his armor in the long, dark hours before starting out on his first quest.

Presently, overcome by weariness, he went to bed. The thoughts and visions and hopes swirling around in his head grew nebulous and confused, cleared, and grew nebulous again. Sleep took him, and as he slept he dreamed. His dream, like all dreams, was confused in its own logic but it related to a happy time in Geordie's life.

He was smaller and younger then, in those days, a boy in knickerbockers and a Norfolk jacket, with a long black stockings and a Buster Brown collar on his shirt, and he and his father were on a train. They had gotten on it after it had pulled into the depot behind the engine, a great, exciting, roaring iron monster wreathed in steam, shining with brass, clanging a bell and shaking the world. He had almost been afraid of it, and caught his father's hand. The engineer, a superior being high above them in his cab, raised a grimy paw in greeting and made them kin.

The journey to St. Louis was not a long one, but exciting because it was Geordie's first train ride. He had settled down by the time they reached the city, when excitement began anew. His first sight of the Mississippi and the great paddle wheel steamers, the bustle and traffic, and finally the Terminal Hotel kept his eyes wide and his head swiveling. They went into the dining room for lunch; against a background of gleaming linen, shining silver, and great chandeliers he saw his first Negroes, in fancy black suits. The sight of them stopped him at the door.

"Dad!" he said, in a stage whisper. "Dad! They're

black! What's the matter with them, Dad? Why have they turned black?"

Alfred Sutton smiled; he often smiled at Geordie in those days, or put a warm and reassuring arm around him. He put his arm around the boy now, and stooped to whisper to him. "They're Negroes, Geordie. All Negroes are black. They come from Africa, where the sun's very hot all the time. Perhaps they were slaves, or their fathers were. You've read about slaves, or heard people talk about them."

"Yes, sir. I guess I forgot," Geordie said, pretending that he had known about Negroes all the time. Nevertheless, for a little while he kept his father between himself and any black man who drew near them, until their first strangeness had worn off.

That evening his father took him to a show; after the few very amateurish theatricals he had seen the big theatre, the crowd and the music and the show itself, a road company's production of "The Chocolate Soldier," enthralled him so much that he had to crawl into his father's bed and talk about it all and ask questions until he fell asleep.

The next day they took a train for the west, for Geordie's father was going to Denver to look into a company in which he was thinking of investing some money. The sleeping car in which they traveled was another wonder, and by the time Geordie had investigated it to his own satisfaction, toured the train, and even talked at some length to several of the Negro porters the country was beginning to change and demand his attention. Watercourses became fewer, there were dry streambeds, the land grew more arid and the vegetation changed; occasionally they passed big prairie dog villages or saw a few antelope in the distance; presently, like clouds on the horizon, the Rockies began to take shape and as they grew closer gained solidity and thrust their great serrated peaks into the sky.

They were the first mountains that Geordie had ever seen, and he couldn't get enough of looking at them. Patched on the heights with snow, changing with every change of light, their vast rugged sweep, their shadowy canyons and bold shoulders and ridges somehow moved him almost to tears. He couldn't explain it, although he tried; his father tried to help him express himself and told great stories of pioneers, of mountain men, trappers, Indians, and seekers for gold. Alfred Sutton was a good storyteller; the warm simplicity of their relatonship and Geordie's interest and obvious admiration of his knowledge made him a better one. He filled the boy's head with wonderful tales, a thing for which there had never been a consistent opportunity in the busy, day-to-day life at home. Their companionship, so intimate and uninterrupted, made a magic circle around them that excluded all the usual distractions. By the time they got off the train in Denver, with the mountains so close and mysterious, hiding many wonders and colored by the bits of history he had learned, Geordie's affection and respect for his father was far greater than most men ever know from their sons.

This increased as the days went on. Geordie was introduced to the men Alfred Sutton had come to see. He sat quietly at their conferences, and it was very evident to him that his father was held in great respect and esteem; he had a presence that always set him a little apart. Geordie was very proud of this, but glad when the talks were over and he had his father to himself again and they could wander a little more before they started home.

They went to Colorado Springs, where Alfred Sutton rented a horse and surrey with a fringed top and a driver to take them out to the Garden of the Gods, and drove about among the great strange red sandstone formations that seemed to make of the place a different little world tucked in against the rise of the Front Range, and took the Moffat Road train around the Georgetown Loop.

This, to Geordie, was the best of all because it was in the wonderful mountains themselves. The endless evergreen forests, the white water of mountain streams, the spidery, scary trestles and the vast, ever-widening views as the train climbed upward was a source of endless fascination to a young flatlander. They climbed higher, to timberline where trees grew stunted and scattered and finally fell away and tiny, flowered plants took their place, into the snows of the summits where the air was thin and cold and it seemed that the whole world was spread below them.

They were among the evergreens again, on the way down, when the train stopped and two wild-looking, bearded men got on. They both carried lever-action rifles, and each had a wildcat skin thrown over his shoulder; they were the very stuff of Alfred Sutton's tales come to life, encountered in an atmosphere that had already strongly moved the boy. They made a tremendous impression upon him (an impression that remained long after it had drifted into the back of his conscious mind), and he caught his father by the arm. "They're trappers, Dad! They're trappers! I want to be a trapper in the mountains like them when I grow up."

Perhaps his perceptions were unusually acute at that moment, for somehow he was aware that his father had withdrawn from him, that their relationship was suddenly in abeyance. His father's expression hardened, and he shook his head. "You wouldn't like their life, Geordie. It's hard and dirty and poor. I think you'd rather be a lawyer, like your Dad."

Geordie recoiled, confused, but before he had time to collect his impressions his father moved swiftly to obliterate them. He smiled again and put an arm around the boy. "You're right," he said. "They're like Jim Bridger and the other mountain men. Aren't we lucky we've seen them? They're like the old times come back again."

Geordie nodded and smiled and snuggled into the encircling arm. The warmth was back again between them and he talked more about the two men; it was not until later, when they were back on the plain and the men had gone, that he half recalled the moment and felt bewildered and alone. This feeling came back to him several times after they got home, and deepened through the years in moments when he recalled the trip. He and his father never recaptured the wonderful closeness again, for there were distractions and other interests and people; Alfred Sutton often talked about the law and Geordie grew ever more interested in the outdoors. Imperceptibly they moved further apart. It was not an alienation but a subtle withdrawal on the part of Alfred Sutton, who probably didn't realize that he was withdrawing as his cherished wish seemed more and more unlikely of fulfillment.

As Geordie's dream moved toward its end he saw the two trappers again against the background of the heights, and then they began to fade. Before the men were quite blotted out, however, a darkness like the shadow of a cloud moved in front of them. The shifting vapor gathered into the form of his father and was outlined in a suffused and glowing light like that emanating from a heroic and beloved figure in an illustrated book of legends. In one hand he held the tablets of the law, which Geordie had seen pictured in the hand of Moses; he extended his free hand beseechingly in Geordie's direction and then he began to recede, to grow smaller and further away. Geordie half awoke and tried to follow him, but could not. He was bound in his place, and couldn't break his bonds. "Dad!" he shouted. "Dad! Don't go away! Wait! Wait for me!"

The two men downstairs heard him and jumped up, scattering the chessmen. They ran up the stairs. Lavinia Sutton, lying sleepless, leaped out of bed and ran toward his room. She reached him first, and had him in her arms when the men got there. He was still not fully awake, twitching as though still trying to follow the figure in his dream.

"It's all right, Geordie," the men at the door heard Lavinia Sutton say. "You were having a nightmare, but it's all right now."

"Dad was going away," he said, calmer as he awoke more fully. "I was dreaming of our trip to the mountains and the trappers on the train, and then he began to go away and I couldn't go with him."

Lavinia Sutton's hands stroked his back, and her look at the men seemed to ask them to go away and leave her with him. They glanced at each other and turned quietly away from the door to go down the stairs again. They didn't speak until they were in the living room.

"Gave me quite a turn," Alfred Sutton said. "It must have been the very devil of a nightmare, for he is old enough now not to be so upset by the usual thing."

"He seems to have felt that he was losing you, Alfred," Uncle Harry said, "You saw those trappers he mentioned on your Denver trip?"

"Yes. He was young then, he said he wanted to be a trapper in the mountains."

"I see," Uncle Harry said. "You must have tried to dissuade him then."

"I did, as a matter of fact. Extraordinary that he should recall all that now, and dream about it."

"Alfred," Uncle Harry said, "don't you see? It's . . . Ah, this is really none of my affair, but do you mind if I say something?" Alfred Sutton shook his head, and Uncle Harry went on. "It's vitally important to him, looking up to you as he does, to feel that he has your complete support if he chooses some other career than the law."

Alfred Sutton looked at the floor for a long moment after this was said, and finally raised his head again. "Harry," he said, "it's good of you to give me your thought on this, and there may be something in what you say. I don't quite agree with you that a life of stuffing things and all that will get him very far. He's young and doesn't realize this yet, but given time I think he will. The entire nation is getting away from this wide open spaces, backwoods sort of thing, developing, industrializing, growing up. I want the best for him, I don't want him left behind like an outdated frontiersman. No, I'll give him more time. He'll see it eventually."

Uncle Harry, realizing the futility of more talk, nodded. "Well," he said, "things seem to have quieted down upstairs, and I'd better be getting on."

"Take the car," Alfred Sutton said. "It was good of you to take them to the lecture. I'm sorry there was such an uproar at the end of it."

"We all enjoyed the lecture," Uncle Harry said. "Geordie, I think, enjoyed it most of all. Good night, Alfred." He nodded and went out the front door, thinking as he walked toward the car that he was all on Geordie's side now and would carry on a guerilla war with Alfred if he had to to help the boy in the direction he wanted to go.

EIGHT

Several evenings later Uncle Harry stopped by with the museum library card. Nothing was said about Geordie's nightmare after the lecture, for Geordie was rather ashamed of making such a scene at his age and didn't really understand why he had done it, and Uncle Harry carefully avoided any conversational gambit that might bring it up. He realized that the boy had been so strongly moved because he had already subconsciously chosen his way; he knew that Geordie wasn't going to have an easy time of it, that he would need support sooner or later, and he intended to lend a hand behind the scenes if and when the opportunity to do so presented itself. He would have to be careful, for he didn't want to alienate his brother-in-law and through him his sister. He didn't like the idea of meddling in the family's affairs, he admitted that Alfred's intentions were of the best, but he felt very strongly that Geordie had the right to choose his own career with a free mind and he hoped that something he might do would bring Alfred around.

The conversation among the four of them was general, and then the two men sat down to play a game of chess. It was too late to go to the library, so Geordie watched the game for awhile with mild interest and went to bed.

He and Spence had planned a trip for the next day, but he was so eager to get to the library that he went to Spence's house after breakfast and asked Spence to excuse him. "I'll go tomorrow if you want," he said. "But I really want to see the library and maybe get a book or two, now that I've got my card."

"You'd better go, I guess, then tomorrow we can go to Ringo's marsh and start building our blind. I can work on the decoys today. They need a little paint."

"You can come to the library with me, if you want."

"I don't think I will," Spence said. He enjoyed watching birds and shooting at some of them, but he didn't want to read about them. "You go ahead."

"All right. I'll get some nails while I'm downtown. We need more nails."

"We need some twine too. Get some of that. I'll see you tomorrow."

"See you tomorrow," Geordie said. He went home, got his bicycle, and rode to MacBride Hall. Instead of going to the library first he climbed to the third floor and went slowly through Mammal Hall and Bird Hall and looked carefully and long at the mounted specimens that he had only glimpsed in the dim light when Dr. Black and Dr.

Satterthwaite had taken them upstairs after the lecture. The museum had a very fine collection for that era; the life of the prairies was very well represented, and Stefansson and several other former students who had been to the Arctic or the tropics or to other parts of the United States had contributed to it, and Satterthwaite's predecessor, Conover, had both contributed to and organized it. Satterthwaite had carried on Conover's work and both of them had brought back specimens from Laysan. As he moved about, looking at all these things, Geordie began to realize the extent of the work and dedication that had gone into their collection and preservation and how important this was for the broadening of man's knowledge of his world. This hadn't occurred to him before because he had never thought of it in that light; what little collecting he had done had been intensely personal, as in the case of the phalarope; the several hours he spent in the museum broadened his outlook considerably.

Finally he went downstairs to the library. Because the fall term hadn't started yet there were only three people there beside the librarian, and he went over to her desk, introduced himself to her, and showed her his card. She was a middle-aged, bright-eyed woman, rather severe looking until she smiled.

"Why, you're Mr. Sutton," she said. "Dr. Satterthwaite said you might be in, and that you were interested in birds. Your uncle was here with him. It's nice that you can get acquainted with the library before the term starts. Can I help you?"

Geordie, secretly pleased to be called "Mr. Sutton" and placed by implication among serious people, gave her his slow grin. "Yes, ma'am," he said. "If you can show me how to find the bird books, I'd appreciate it."

"They're all under 'Ornithology' here," she said, and

got up and took him to the index files. She pulled out a drawer and took it to a table. "There. You can look through it and pick out what you want."

Geordie thanked her, sat down, and began to leaf through the file. He soon discovered that what Uncle Harry had said was true: here were riches far beyond what he had known before. There was so much that he was confused and didn't know what to choose; finally he took the drawer to the librarian's desk.

"I don't know what to start with," he said apologetically. "There's so much."

"You'll very probably be assigned basic and collateral reading when classes start, and they will suggest other things to you. But for now . . . Have you had any zoology, or avian physiology? No? That might be a good place to start." She went through the file, wrote several numbers down, and went with him to show him where to find the books. "Here's the physiology," she said, taking it down. It was a big book; he put it under his arm. She took down another. "This is a sort of introduction to zoology," she said. "You'll have it in your course, but it won't do any harm to look at it now." He took that one too. "You don't have to read them as carefully as though you were preparing for a test, but if you go through them you'll find a lot of interesting things. Read through them, and before you come back again I'll look up some other books for you to take out."

"I sure appreciate your trouble," Geordie said, very pleased to meet someone who was so helpful, and still a little startled that college wasn't, apparently, going to be as stuffy as he had imagined it.

"It's a pleasure to help anyone who is really interested. Dr. Satterthwaite will be in, and I'll ask him to recommend something."

Geordie smiled, thanked her again, and went out. By

the time he was outside he realized that he didn't even know her name. She was so different from the rather crabbed librarian he was used to, who seemed to find everything a chore, that she had confused him a little. In fact, the whole day so far had confused him a little and exhilarated him too, because it had made him feel a part of a serious and important enterprise rather than a boy whose inclination interested few people besides himself. He was so preoccupied thinking of this that he was half-way home before he remembered the nails and twine and had to go back for them.

He was so late that he missed his lunch, but Ingrid gave him some doughnuts and milk in the kitchen; then he went up to his room and spent the rest of the afternoon with the two books. He looked through the one on zoology first and decided to come back to it; he put it aside and curled up in one of the upholstered chairs with the other. There were many words in it that he didn't know; some he looked up in the dictionary and some he blundered over, guessing at the sense from the context. He went at it in a rush, like a hungry man bolting his food, knowing that he would read it again more carefully, but despite his haste he began to see how wonderfully birds were made for their function. He had known a little, but not much; the day of books that popularized such subjects had not yet come. He read on, fascinated.

The two boys finished working on their blind for the duck shooting season, and the fall term began at the University. Geordie managed to arrange most of his classes in the mornings, and so looked forward to several free afternoons a week when he could get out and wander about. Spence, who would be working toward an engineering degree, managed to hold out one afternoon a week besides Saturday, so they would in a measure be able to go together. The business of learning their way around, beginning classes, and settling into the routine of their new life occupied them for a time.

Geordie's favorite subject from the first was Biology, and Satterthwaite, who taught it, his favorite teacher. Other professors might occasionally have lapses into boredom but Satterthwaite had an unflagging enthusiasm for the science of life and its endless ramifications and mysteries. He was full of observations made on his various trips, and told many stories of his experiences. A number of these were hilarious, for he was a lively and inquisitive traveler without self-consciousness, and didn't mind laughing at himself over his misadventures. Lean and bald, restless, good-natured, talking in little bursts and occasionally stabbing out with a finger as Geordie had first seen him at the Laysan lecture, he led them on. Listening to him, Geordie was often very thankful that he had quietly held out for Biology when he and his father had gone over the curriculum and picked his subjects. "Biology?" his father had asked, without enthusiasm. "Are you quite sure?"

"Yes, sir. I'd like to take it."

"I understand it's rather messy, cutting up frogs and things. Why do you want to do that?"

"I want to know what makes them work," Geordie had said.

"Do you think you can come at the spirit or the life of the brain by watching a beating heart or examining a section of muscle? This seems to me to be trying to get at a mystery by cataloguing the mechanics."

This had been rather unfair, a tactic to confuse, but

Geordie had not been drawn by it. "Yes, sir. I guess it is, but I'd like to take it anyhow."

"If you wish, then. If it turns out to be unsatisfactory, you can change to something else next year."

As he worked on his zoology experiments Geordie often thought of his father's comment, and the more he learned of life processes the more wonderful the fact of life itself, beyond its mechanics, became to him. This was not the case with some of his fellow students, who were gradually turning into mechanists pure and simple, and there were many arguments in what they called 'bull sessions' outside of class. The mechanists were the more vocal and had concrete examples on their side with which they pelted the non-mechanists, who tended to go off into intangibles and lose themselves. Geordie would listen to these wrangles for a time, grin, and go off to the library; both sides got a good deal of mental exercise but neither ever convinced the other and he, Geordie, preferred to learn more about the habits and personalities of the birds and animals. The mechanists, he thought, would be laboratory men, researchers, who would make many valuable contributions which were greatly needed; he intended to become firmly based in laboratory techniques and then get out into the sun and air and perhaps discover not what a dietary deficiency or a parasite did to to a blue-winged teal but how and why it migrated.

Migration was particularly on his mind just then because he and Spence, on their days afield together, were seeing the beginning of it. As the leaves blazed in color and the countryside slowly changed from green toward the dry, dun monotone of winter the summer birds were leaving and the birds from further north were beginning to appear, some to pause a little and then leave, and some to stay. Goldenrod, and blue, white, and purple prairie asters (which have since that time largely disappeared with the original grasses), gave their color to the prairie; sunflowers had ripened their seeds and drew the seedeaters, and wild grape and crabapple bore their fruits along the river bluffs among the bright sumacs. Red-tailed hawks on the move drew their ellipses in the sky; blue-winged teal, early migrators, and an occasional boldly patterned avocet appeared in the marshes.

The two boys spent some pre-shooting season time in their blind, content to be lazily sitting in the pleasant autumn sun just watching the life about them. They were pleased to see that their marsh, which they had picked after a long survey of the marshes they knew, seemed to hold up in its attractiveness to birds. When they were pretty sure that they were going to have good shooting Geordie spoke to Dr. Satterthwaite.

"We've watched our marsh for a couple of week-ends," he said, "and it seems to be pretty good. You said at the Laysan lecture that you'd like to shoot with us."

"So I would, so I would. Nice of you to remember me, Geordie. Name your time and I'll be with you."

"You can come any time you want to," Geordie said. "After we show it to you, and how to get there, you could go whenever you wished. I've told Uncle Harry about it. I don't think anybody else knows about it."

"I'm already licking my chops," Dr. Satterthwaite said. "Incidentally, you'd better call me Doc out of class. I can foresee difficulty if you have to say: 'Dr. Satterthwaite, sir, there's a mallard approaching from the left.' Don't you agree?"

Geordie grinned. "Yes, sir."

"Can I give you a hand building the blind?"

"We've built it, and painted the decoys. All you have to do is come."

"Better and better. I'll always arrange to bring the lunches, then, when I come."

"Well," Geordie said, "I don't think you have to. I usually cook a little something."

Satterthwaite's look seemed to sharpen a little. "It will be a little hard to get used to all this luxury. Why did you turn into a cook?"

"I got tired of cold sandwiches, I guess, and then I watched Ingrid a couple of times. Ingrid's our cook."

"I hear from your uncle that she's a phenomenon. It will be great fun to shoot with you and Harry. I had a sort of running competition with him last year." The finger came out. "He beat me by five ducks. This year it'll be different."

"Could you come on opening day?" Geordie asked.

"Greater love hath no man," Satterthwaite said, "than to share the opening day with a friend. I'll have to give you a good term mark." He grinned. "I'll have to anyhow if you continue the good work. You're doing very well, you know." The finger transfixed him. "See that you don't slow down."

"No, sir," Geordie said, mightily pleased. "I won't."

"I know it's probably too soon to tell, but do you have any idea yet what you want to do? I guess it's inevitable as we learn more, but biology seems to be dividing into specialities. Have you any indication at all what you would like yours to be?"

Somehow it seemed to Geordie that there was some reason for the question beyond the interest that Satterthwaite had always shown in the plans and interests of his students. He didn't know what this reason could be, and couldn't guess. "I like birds best," he said, "but I don't think I'd like to do laboratory research on them. I'd rather be out where they are."

"An ornithologist, then, a field ornithologist. Good, very good. We'll see what kind of a cook you are."

He grinned again and managed to look mysterious; Geordie felt a stirring of excitement, for he was sure there was something behind all this. Perhaps it was a field trip, maybe into country he didn't know; he would love to take a field trip with Satterthwaite. His curiosity got the better of him. "Dr. Satterthwaite—"

"Doc."

"Doc, then. Do you have some reason for asking?"

"I should hope I had a reason for every question I asked," Satterthwaite said, and began to gather up his papers. "I've got to go. Stop in my office tomorrow afternoon and we'll make our shooting arrangements."

"All right," Geordie said, grinned, and went out of the room. He almost felt like skipping. Something was in the wind; something was surely in the wind.

NINE

The week-end before the season opened Geordie and Spence made a trip to the marsh, to take the decoys and a Dutch oven. Geordie, after conferring with Ingrid, decided that he would use it to make a fine stew, for Doc, as he was trying to get into the habit of calling Satterthwaite, had put such a mysterious emphasis on cooking that he wanted to impress him. It was a heavy thing to carry, and he hoped that lugging it along would turn out to be worth the trouble.

"Good Christmas!" Spence had said, when he first saw it. "You'll break your back with that thing. What do you want to take it for?"

"I want to give Doc a real good lunch. He's got something up his sleeve. Besides, we can leave it there and use it again. They have another one here. I'll carry it."

"I'll carry it halfway," Spence said, "but the lunch better be good."

They set out in the brakecart; when they reached the point on the road opposite the marsh they could drive a way across the prairie, but the last half mile or so they had to walk. They were both tired of the Dutch oven by the time they got there, but were cheered by the number of ducks that took to the air as they approached.

"There are a lot of them using the marsh," Geordie said, with satisfaction. "It's going to be all right. It ought to get better as more of them come down."

They dropped their gear and made another trip to get all the decoys from the cart, and then put on their boots and took all the stuff they had brought out to the island where they had built the blind. It was a long, narrow island several hundred yards from shore, with some medium-height swamp oaks, sycamores, and other trees and a good deal of head-high brush on it; the blind was on the northern point with plenty of water in front of it. They put the decoys and the oven in the blind, and walked back sixty or seventy yards into the brush and gathered enough wood for a fire. Geordie's idea was to do the cooking there, away from the blind, among a few trees that would give some concealment. The brush would give them pretty good cover as they moved back and forth between the fire and the blind.

Because it couldn't be seen from any road and was unsuspected by most people, the little marsh, which wasn't more than twenty or thirty acres in extent, hadn't been shot or disturbed, so far as the boys knew, for a long time. No one who hadn't wandered widely over the country, as they had, would have known it was there, and they looked upon it as a secret place. It was shallow, with no stream flowing out of it to be followed up, and had a good growth of aquatic plants. Quite a few ducks nested on the island in the spring, and other birds, for the water surrounding it kept off weasels, wandering dogs, and other nest disturbers.

The two boys got through their chores and left as quickly as they could, so as not to scare any of the ducks they had flushed that might want to return for the night. They returned to Geordie's house where Spence spent the night.

The long-awaited morning finally came, and the two boys were shaken from sleep in the small hours by the alarm clock. They both staggered to the window and saw that it was very dark, overcast, and windy—a good day to keep ducks on the move. They sleepily congratulated each other, dressed, and went down to the kitchen, where Ingrid had left a bag holding the ingredients of a stew. By the time breakfast was ready they were wide awake. They had just finished eating when Uncle Harry and Doc came in, booted, bundled to the ears and bright-eyed with anticipation, to be followed shortly by Laverty, who was to drive them out and come back for them at the end of the day.

"God bless all here," he said, touching his forelock with exaggerated humility, "and may you be slaughtering a great lot of the poor ducks."

"It's nice to have your blessing," Uncle Harry said, grinning at him. "Can you keep up your good works and take a little of the chill off the day? It's too cold for this time of year."

"I'll try, sir, I'll try, but I can smell a bit of snow on the way, God forbid."

"Amen," Uncle Harry said, and looked at his watch. "It's time to go."

Geordie and Spence put on their boots and got their guns and shells, and Geordie picked up the bag; they all went out into the cold and windy dark, and climbed into the carriage. Laverty clucked to Uncle Harry's horse, and they set out. The carriage curtains were up and rattled in the wind; they pulled the buffalo robes up to their chins and snuggled into them. Geordie sat up front with Laverty, to direct him, and almost missed the turn-off point onto the prairie in the dark, but finally they reached the end of the ride and started on the walk after arranging with Laverty to check in the middle of the day to see if they wanted to leave then. The wind buffeted them and brought tears to their eyes, but a slowly mounting excitement kept them warm. There was a skim of ice on the water, and as it broke around them with a crackle there was a roar of wings and a great cackling as the sleeping ducks awoke and took off.

Fortunately the area before the blind had been in the wind's lee and the ducks had bunched there and kept the water open; it was a good omen. All four of them sloshed about and set out the decoys and then got into the blind out of the wind, to blow on their fingers and stamp their feet. Presently the first faint, suffused glow of sunrise appeared in the east and slowly began to spread, dyeing the overcast and setting the edges of the clouds on fire. They heard several ducks which they couldn't see return and splash down, talking to each other.

Geordie loved this hour of the day when he could watch the world emerge from night and open out toward the horizon; he loved the silence, the changing light, and life beginning to stir again. The sky was taking on more color and soon the ducks would begin to come in, but he tore himself away and went back into the brush to start the fire and put on the stew. There was a stirring in the brush as he went, a mink or a coon moving away from him to hole up for the day, and there was the dark and silent shadow against the paling sky of an owl on the move, glimpsed and gone. He started the fire, got some water in the oven, dumped the ingredients in, and set the oven on to cook. As he turned away to return four ducks came over him, their wings set, to swing into the decoys. They would be the first of the day, and he wouldn't be there; he stood and waited for the guns, but they didn't speak. Something had alerted the ducks, and they must have gone off. When he stepped into the blind again everybody was laughing.

"What happened?" he asked.

"We were all sitting down," Spence said. "Uncle Harry stood up for a look just as some ducks came in. He scared them, and they kept right on going."

"They didn't even pause to say good-bye," Uncle Harry said ruefully. "Just for that, I'll be sentinel."

He stood up in his corner of the blind to watch; the light grew stronger, and in a while Uncle Harry crouched down a little.

"Bunch coming," he said. "Keep low, and get set."

Excitement caught them all; they picked up their guns and their muscles tensed. They crouched, ready to jump up, trembling a little; they couldn't see, but could imagine, the ducks coming closer, closer . . .

"They're dropping," Uncle Harry whispered, reaching one hand out for his gun. "Dropping. They'll come in right in front. Eight or ten . . . Now!"

They all jumped up. Uncle Harry had timed it very well; the ducks, blue-winged teal, were just dropping their feet and backing their wings. Geordie picked out a drake and pulled the trigger, but nothing happened. The guns on each side of him opened up and several teal fell, and Geordie followed the flaring drake and pulled the rear trigger and nothing happened again except the click of the firing pin on an empty chamber as the flock scudded over them. In his preoccupation with the sunrise and the stew he had forgotten to load his gun. Disappointment and mortification turned him brick red; he sat down quickly, hoping to escape attention, but they were all looking at him with wide grins and nudging each other: they had all heard the last click.

"Very quiet gun you've got there," Uncle Harry said.

"Certainly is an improvement over these noisy things we shoot," Doc said. "Just a little click."

"Sort of a conservation measure."

"We'll have to tell people about it," Doc said, and they all laughed immoderately.

Geordie sat and took it, and finally even he began to grin. "I'll do better next time," he said, and loaded his gun. "I'll get the ducks." He waded out and picked up three ducks, and brought them in. In his absence they'd elected him watchman for his sins, and he changed places with Uncle Harry and stood with his head under the roof of the blind, back in the corner out of the wind.

It was full light now, or as light as it was going to be with the overcast, and there was still color in the sky; Geordie saw a marsh hawk beyond the water working its beat, rising and dropping on the wind. Four crows went by to the east, and then beyond them Geordie saw a single duck materialize against the gray sky. It was coming for them and he decided to get even with the other three by not saying anything and shooting it himself. The duck rapidly drew closer, began to swing away, saw the decoys, and swung toward them again. Geordie tensed, ready to grab his gun; there was an undertone of conversation beside him, and despite his concentration on the approaching duck he heard Doc say: ". . . and I've been in correspondence with the Biological Survey about a trip to shoot all the rabbits, and it is beginning to look as though something might . . ."

Laysan! he thought. *It's Laysan he's talking about! If he's going to Laysan he might be thinking of taking me!* The duck, a drake mallard, was almost in the decoys and setting itself to land; Geordie grabbed up his gun and shot at it. His concentration, however, had been so shattered by what he had heard that he missed it completely. It swung off the other end of the blind. Everybody jumped up and Doc, who was in that corner, swung and shot. It was a very long shot, but successful; the duck went down in a long glide and fell on the prairie beyond the edge of the marsh.

Everybody was looking at Geordie again, and Doc was grinning like the Cheshire cat. "I was going to get even with you all," Geordie said, to explain himself. "It was a single, and I thought I'd . . . I . . ."

"The vindictive type," Uncle Harry said and laughed. "Hoist with his own petard, he was." They were all laughing at him again, even Spence. "Well, my boy," Uncle Harry went on. "For the good of your soul, you can go get the duck. It will teach you to try to take a mean advantage of your trusting friends."

"Yes, sir," Geordie said. "I guess I'd better go get it. Spence, will you check the water in the stew, and build up the fire?"

Spence nodded, and Geordie crawled out of the blind and waded ashore. His head was full of wild surmises as he went, buffeted by the wind, and equally wild schemes as to how he could find out from Doc if there was any connection between the sentence he had heard in the blind and the questions Doc had asked him a week or so before. He was fully aware that there would be no real reason to take him, for he had nothing to offer. But still . . .

By the time he had reached the mallard, and settled down somewhat, he knew there was no way to ask Doc. It would not only be very presumptious, it would be stupid, for when he had tried it before he had gotten no real answer. He would just have to wait, and hope, and maybe he would see. He picked up the mallard, and as he turned toward the blind to start back he saw a flock of ducks come in and several splashes and then heard the rumble of the guns.

After a start that left something to be desired, Geordie's day began to improve. To his delight, he killed a duck that Doc had missed with both barrels, and then three others before the morning flights began to slow down. Everybody had done well, and they had had a fine time and collected a good bunch of ducks. They were all very happy with the little marsh, lonely and quiet as it was, with no one else anywhere in sight to disturb the ducks that were coming in. "Maybe we don't know how lucky we are," Doc said, in one of the lulls. "I have a notion that in a few years it's going to be very hard to find a modest little earthly paradise like this without owning miles of country. You two boys certainly did a fine job when you found it. I appreciate very much being let in on it."

"So do I," Uncle Harry said. "And I'm going to appreciate the lunch, for every once in awhile I get a drift of fragrance on the wind that makes my mouth water. Do we have to wait much longer? I had breakfast awfully early."

"It ought to be about ready now," Geordie said. He had been back to the fire several times, and when he had tasted the stew he had been very pleased with it. He and Spence now took the oven off the fire, put on the battered coffee pot, and brought the oven back to the blind swinging on a pole they carried between them. When the top was taken off a wonderful fragrance filled the blind, for Ingrid had helped Geordie add the spices. Doc and Uncle Harry exchanged happy glances. They handed out the tin plates and spoons, gave everybody a big hunk of bread, and fell to. After the first mouthful Doc sat chewing with his eyes on Geordie; there was an abstracted expression in them. Suddenly he blinked, his eyes focused again, he took another spoonful, and a wide smile appeared on his face. "Well, Harry," he said, "you told me, but you sold the boy short. Geordie, I'm your man. Any time you want to go shooting, just whistle." He thrust out the finger. "Or just look like you're going to."

"Yes, sir," Geordie said. He was very pleased, and more hopeful now that he might be chosen for whatever mysterious enterprise (for he was sure there was something) that Doc had in mind. "I like to shoot with you too. I get a nice chance to pick up a duck once in awhile."

"You do, do you? Harry, would you say that this rising generation fails a little in respect?"

"No," Uncle Harry said. "And stop worrying about your ego when your real worry's marksmanship. Eat your stew, man, before it freezes over."

Doc grinned and returned to his stew. After they had all finished they washed the spoons and plates and the oven, and sat outside near the blind drinking their coffee. Out of the wind and warmed by the splendid meal, they were content; a great and happy peace descended upon them.

"Laverty's coming back in a while, isn't he?" Uncle Harry asked presently.

"Yes; he is."

"Why don't we knock off and go with him? We have enough ducks, we don't want to shoot them all. If we get out now they won't be disturbed when they return, and that will make it better another day."

"Yes, sir, I think that would be fine."

"Agreed," Doc said. "Besides," he went on, pointing to the north, "it looks like snow over there. If—"

What he was going to say was never finished, for off in the distance, coming mellowly down the wind, there were the voices of geese. Like a family of groundhogs all trying to pop into the same burrow they scrambled wildly over each other getting back into the blind, sorted themselves out, and inched up their heads cautiously to peer through the reeds covering the front. Spence saw them first.

"Northwest!" he said. "They're turning! They've seen the marsh! they're coming!"

They scarcely breathed; the almost ecstatic excitement aroused in any hunter by approaching geese made them all tremble, but outwardly they were as still as stones. The big wedge, gabbling, swung into the wind, broke formation, and set their wings. The geese looked huge, and beautiful.

"One apiece," Uncle Harry said. "Now!"

Four geese fell, and with a great crying and beating of wings the rest swung and rose away on the wind. The four people in the blind pounded each other with exclamations of vast pleasure, and as he and Spence started out of the blind to pick up the geese Geordie saw the tiny figure of Laverty coming toward them far across the distant prairie. If he had come a few minutes earlier the geese would have swung away.

TEN

Doc had enjoyed the opening day so much, and was so appreciative, that Geordie soon asked him to go again; from this they fell into shooting together a good deal. Their schedules were somewhat similar in free time, they got along well together, and they both benefited. Geordie had wandered so widely that he knew a great deal more of the country than a busy man could have found out for himself, and this gave Doc better hunting; the association was certainly good for Geordie. There might have been a suspicion of an ulterior motive at first in his cultivation of Doc; he was always on the alert to hear more of Doc's plans and tried to ingratiate himself, but a genuine and increasing liking for the man soon took the place of this. It wouldn't have lasted on any other basis anyhow; Geordie was too honest for ulterior motives to hold him for long, and if he hadn't liked Doc he would soon have avoided him no matter what.

Sometimes they hunted prairie chickens or sharp-tailed grouse, but they spent more hours after ducks either in the marsh or along the river. Hidden in the blind or sitting quietly in the boat in the reeds along a bank of the river or one of the creeks or backwaters that opened into it they saw more. They were both endlessly interested in observing the actions and habits of wildlife and could be perfectly content to spend hours doing it; this made them even more agreeable to each other, and occasionally enabled them to pick up an unusual specimen for the Museum or one that had strayed from its usual range.

One day in the blind Geordie was on watch and caught out of the corner of his eye a pale, swift bird quartering past. He didn't recognize it, but reacted quickly; he grabbed his gun and shot. The bird fell, and when he retrieved it Doc identified it as a prairie falcon. "A partial albino," he said, "and well east of its range. It might be the first one recorded in Iowa. Very interesting. For some reason the Museum doesn't have one, and they'll be delighted to get it. If it is a first record, you'll be famous forever. Among a few people, that is. Incidentally, the museum course starts pretty soon. They've finally got the details straightened out. Are you still going to take it?"

"Yes, sir."

"I don't know whether I see you as a museum man or not. Like me, you like to waste too much time sitting in the bushes. Have you thought about that?"

"Yes. It's fun sitting in the bushes. Besides, we get a specimen once in awhile. If I'm going to be a naturalist I think I ought to take the course. I ought to know as much as I can. If I'm going to get specimens, I ought to know the best way to prepare them."

"That's sensible," Doc said, and stuck out the finger. "Why did you say 'If I'm going to be a naturalist'? Is there any doubt in your mind?"

Geordie was silent for a moment. "My father wants me to be a lawyer," he said finally, "and I . . . Well, he wants so much for me to be a lawyer. He's always wanted me to. He says that the country is developing so fast that sooner or later there won't be anything for naturalists to do. Do you believe that, Doc?"

Doc shook his head. "We haven't got very far," he said. "We believed in spontaneous generation until about forty years ago, we haven't known about viruses for more than eighteen or twenty. We don't even know very much about bird migration, which goes on around us all the time. The American Bird Banding Association, that might well give us very valuable information in a few years, was only organized two or three years ago. We've got a long way to go, and I think naturalists will be cutting trails for quite a time. Natural history, which is branching into all sorts of specialties, will tell us more and more about our world and life itself." He paused, and grinned. "I can't advise you what your life's work will be. You'll have to decide that for yourself. But don't think there won't be enough to do, well beyond your lifetime."

About a week later Uncle Harry was able to join them for the day. Geordie and Doc had used the blind two days before, and as they didn't like to use it too frequently they decided to shoot a backwater several miles down the river. A little way into its wandering course they rounded a corner and came upon Possum. Possum's back was toward them; he was leaning over the side of his boat, pulling at something. As Doc said later, he must have had eyes in the back of his head, for although they hadn't made a sound he ceased what he was doing, straightened up, and faced them with an air of surprise and innocence. He was as hairy and unkempt as ever, and his chin was brown with tobacco juice.

"Hi, boy," he said to Geordie, and gave a casual and all-inclusive nod. "You ever hear from that warden?"

Geordie stared at him, nonplussed; he didn't know what to say for a moment. He looked from one of his companions to the other, and found both their glances upon him. "No," he managed to say, finally. "No, I didn't." He lapsed into silence again, confused by Possum's treachery in airing the secret.

"That's good," Possum said. "That's real good." He picked up his oars. "Lost my tonic, and I ain't been able to find it. I got to git along. I been seein' ducks come in about a half mile back up yonder. You ought to git up there." He nodded again, bent to the oars, and was soon out of sight around the bend in the backwater.

Geordie bent to the oars too, anxious to be under way and to provide some distraction; Uncle Harry, who was also rowing, held off a few strokes and then began to row too. There was a silence in the boat. They moved out of the reach and presently got into the one that Possum had indicated; there wasn't a duck in sight. Both Geordie and Uncle Harry shipped their oars.

"He seemed mighty anxious to get us out of there," Uncle Harry said, "now that I think of it. Didn't you think so, Geordie?"

"Yes, sir," Geordie said unhappily. He was aware by

now that neither of them was going to question him directly but that they were both very curious. "I . . ." he said. "I don't know why he said what he did about the warden." Another silence greeted this, and Geordie saw that he was going to have to tell them. He blushed to the roots of his hair, and then stumbled through the story of Possum and the dynamite and the warden. "I thought he was just going fishing," he said. "And then after I got in the boat I couldn't get out. I thought the warden would tell my father, so I told him—the warden—that I hadn't seen him." He blushed again, and then felt greatly relieved that the story was out.

They were both smiling at him now, and Doc said: "The old ruffian's smarter than I thought he was. He was up to something, and decided that coming up with the warden business would distract us enough so that we wouldn't wonder about it or ask him what he was doing."

"I wonder what he was up to?" Uncle Harry asked. "He was pulling something up. What would he be doing that for, Sat?"

"I don't know, I can't . . . Wait a minute. I wonder if he has a sunken net in that reach, to catch ducks that might be searching around under water? I'll bet that was it, the old devil. Maybe he's thrown some corn in there, so that any ducks that dive for it would be caught and drown. By Christopher! Let's go back and see! If that's what he was doing, we can put him away for awhile."

This made Geordie unhappy once more. "Doc," he said. "Doc, if we get him arrested he'll go to my father to get him out. He always does. And if he tells about the warden . . ."

"Ah, me," Doc said. "Now you can see what evil courses can bring you to. Tangled webs, and all that."

"Besides," Uncle Harry said, "he probably went back

there as soon as we were out of sight and took up the net, if he has one. That's why he wanted to send us up here."

"You seem to know his habits," Doc said. "Do you have a history of law-breaking and encounters with the warden too? Maybe it runs in the family."

"Everybody knows about Possum," Uncle Harry said. "He must be into me for twenty-five or thirty dollars. When he's really up against it, and can't find some law to break, he comes to me for a loan. His stories are so ingenious I always give him one."

Doc threw up his hands. "I'll say no more," he said. "We can't persecute this old friend of the family. He's got something on everybody. I'll go back to my ivory tower. Meantime, where can we get a few shots?"

"Maybe there would be some ducks up near the end of the backwater," Geordie said. "It's almost a mile, but there always used to be ducks there. There are a lot of muskrats there and they've thinned out the cattails enough so that the ducks like it."

"You're a naturalist already," Doc said. "Come back here and let me row awhile. You need a little peace and quiet to organize your conscience."

Geordie changed places with him, and they went on up the reach.

Geordie had been right; there were ducks at the head of the backwater, more came in occasionally, and they had a good afternoon. On the way out they stopped where they had encountered Possum and searched for signs of a net, but could find nothing.

Later, the two men dropped Geordie at his house, and after they had left there and were halfway to the University Satterthwaite said: "Harry, I think the Laysan trip is going to come off, and I'd like to take Geordie along."

"It would certainly be wonderful for Geordie, but why would you want him? He's no scientist yet."

"It's not really a very scientific trip. In view of what Conover and I both found on our trips I've got the Biological Survey thinking that it would be a good thing if a small party went out, shot all the rabbits, collected some more bird skins before some of the birds disappear, and make some observations. The most important thing is to get rid of the rabbits, if there's to be any of the island left. The Survey doesn't have the personnel to do it, but they want it done, and they can get us a little Government money and give us transportation."

"A pretty elaborate rabbit hunt," Uncle Harry said.

"Don't you see the—"

"I do see the importance of it," Uncle Harry said, "if we want to keep some unique species. I'm all for it. But where does Geordie come in?"

"There will only be four or five of us—ornithologists and such. There's usually a promising student or two to lend a hand with the incidental work—collecting, skinning, preserving skins, work around camp. Geordie would fit in fine. He's certainly a promising student, he's a good shot and—last but not least—he's a darn good cook. Have you ever spent a month or so on a deserted island with a poor cook?"

"I didn't realize you were such a sybarite," Uncle Harry said.

"Sybarite be hanged!" Satterthwaite said with some heat, and then laughed. "Stop pulling my leg. It's a question of survival. I've eaten enough bad food on these trips to choke a vulture, and I see a chance to avoid it this time."

They pulled up in front of Satterthwaite's house; Uncle Harry stopped the engine, but neither of them made a move to get out.

"The reason I'm discussing it with you," Satterthwaite said, "is this: do you think his family would let him go?"

"Why do you ask that?"

"Something he said. Something about his father wanting him to be a lawyer. It seemed to bother him, to make him unsure about what he ultimately wants to be. I'll be frank with you, Harry. If he's going to be a naturalist the trip would be very valuable to him; if he's not, it would just be a ride. It wouldn't be fair to some other kid who's going to be a naturalist to take Geordie just because he can cook."

Uncle Harry was silent for a moment. "I'll be frank with you too," he said finally. "There is a conflict. The boy wants more than anything else to be a naturalist. It's all he wants to be, and I don't know why my brother-in-law doesn't let him go his own way. Alfred keeps a little pressure on him a good deal of the time, and because he loves and respects Alfred he's stirred up quite a bit. I brought him to your Laysan lecture just to see if I could strengthen him in his effort to break away."

"You're with him, then."

"I'm with him all the way, although it's really none of my affair. I'm an intruder in a family matter."

"I think you're right, blast it. I'm with him too. I've seldom seen a kid I wanted so much to be a naturalist. He'd be wasted as a lawyer. Well, what will we do?"

"The question will have to be put to Alfred sooner or later," Uncle Harry said, "and as we aren't sure which way Alfred will jump, we'd better see if we can arrange the direction beforehand."

"I didn't realize you were such a Machiavellian type," Satterthwaite said. "Have you got some scheme all laid out?"

"Not yet, but I have a glimmer. I have a feeling that if

Geordie gets to Laysan his conflict will finally straighten out."

"It would help, I'm sure," Satterthwaite said. "But what's the glimmer? Can I take a hand in it?"

"Not yet. But something happened today that might be useful."

"I can't recall anything unusual happening, except that foul old reprobate. What was his name?"

"Possum."

"That's it. It has to do with Possum?"

"We'll see," Uncle Harry said.

"So. A pretty frail reed, I'd say, but any stick will do to beat a dog with." He bestirred himself. "It's my bed time," he said, and got out of the car. "It was a good day. Good night, Harry."

"Good night, Sat. Give the crank a twist on your way past the front of the car."

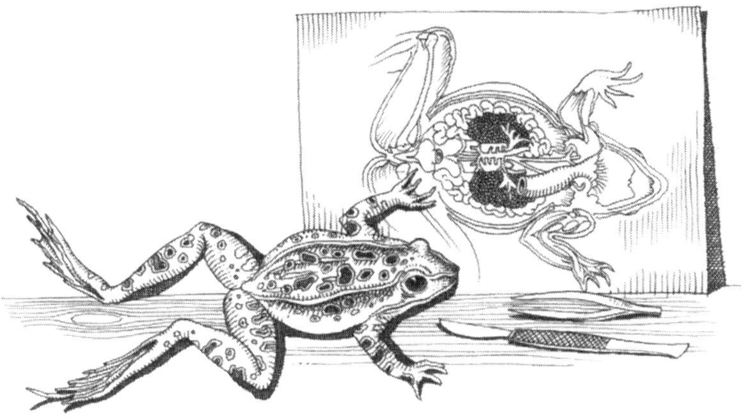

ELEVEN

As Geordie's classes started and he went about dissecting his frogs steeped in formaldehyde and struggling with taxonomy, the museum class began and he was soon in the midst of the details of taxidermy, the making of foregrounds, and the elements of art as it served for backgrounds and arrangement. Dr. Black, as he said himself, was a very poor artist but a pretty good photographer, and Geordie began to learn something about photography from him. He saw the importance of photography at once, and was surprised that he hadn't been taking pictures for some time.

"I don't know why I didn't do it sooner," he said to Doc one day in his office. "Dr. Black doesn't have a picture of an Eskimo curlew, for instance, and now there don't seem to be any to take pictures of. I saw a few in the spring once, and I could have had a picture."

"I could have had pictures of them when a flock would cover a fifty acre field," Doc said, "and that wasn't so long ago either. Back around '93 or '94, I think it was, when I was in Kansas one April. I could have even had a picture of the last whooping crane nest in Iowa, back in '94, but who thought then that it would be the last one? I wasn't as big a fool as a lot of people were, thinking that these birds and animals would last forever at the rate they were being shot, but . . . besides, it was a cumbersome business to take pictures then."

"You took a lot on Laysan," Geordie said.

"I take a lot when I go somewhere else. I hardly ever take any around here. But now that you've got interested you ought to work at it. For practice, if nothing else. You're learning how to develop them too, I take it?"

"Yes, sir, I'm learning all I can," Geordie said, and added: "Sometime I may go somewhere too."

Doc's finger shot out. "Do you want to?"

"Anywhere. Anytime. I used to dream about going to Africa, or India."

"Where do you dream of going now?"

Geordie looked at him for a moment and then decided to say it, come what may. "I dream about going to Laysan."

Doc nodded, and considered him. "Why?" he asked finally, and the finger came out again.

Not many months ago Geordie, feeling the inferiority that all boys feel in the presence of their elders whether they admit it to themselves or not, would have stammered out something inadequate, but a change had been taking place within him. Recently, for the first time in his life, he had been accepted as an equal hunting with men; he had been able to take them to good places they wouldn't have found for themselves; and although he had been in college but a short time it had already opened up far wider horizons for him and given him a sense of purpose. He was, rather suddenly, more mature. The way he had stood up to his father about his choice of courses had been an early sign of this. "Why," he said, "I guess I'd like to go there for the same reason you wanted to go."

"Bravo," Satterthwaite said.

"I heard you say something to Uncle Harry in the blind about getting rid of the rabbits," Geordie said.

"H'm. So you've been laying for me ever since."

Geordie grinned. "Yes, sir."

Satterthwaite did not hide his pleasure. The more Geordie revealed himself the better Satterthwaite liked him; his only reservation now was whether the boy would eventually follow the course he had set out upon or whether, finally, he would be influenced by his father. Satterthwaite wondered whether he was attaching too much importance to this; any one of a number of fortuitous events could occur in the next few years to throw Geordie one way or another and all he had to base his reservation on was what Uncle Harry had told him, but he wanted somehow to assay Geordie's determination. He told himself that he was nit-picking at this juncture, but he had a troublesome feeling of responsibility toward some future scientist that he was unable to sidestep despite his liking for Geordie. He was wondering how to frame a question or two when the door opened and a man's head appeared around it like a head out of a Jack-in-the-box. It was a narrow head, with close-cropped red hair above a narrow, snub-nosed face with a thin mouth.

"Hi, Sat!" it said, and then saw Geordie. The eyes nar-

rowed as though with dislike, and then widened again. "Sorry, I didn't know . . ."

"Come in, John," Satterthwaite said. "Come in."

The man came in. He was tall, and narrow like his face.

"Dr. Catton," Satterthwaite said. "Geordie Sutton, one of my students. A very good one, too."

Geordie ducked his head, smiling, uncertain whether to extend his hand. Dr. Catton settled this question; he nodded coolly and apparently dismissed Geordie from his mind.

"I was on my way north," he said to Satterthwaite, "and thought I'd stop in for a minute to see if the trip was still on the books and progressing."

Satterthwaite didn't reply for a moment; it was evident that he wasn't pleased with the other man's manner. He glanced at Geordie as though in apology and Geordie, seeing nothing but embarrassment for both Doc and himself if he stayed, took a step toward the door. "It was nice to meet you, sir," he said.

"Pleasure," Dr. Catton said, giving him a glance and dismissing him again.

"We'll finish our talk later, Geordie," Satterthwaite said. "We're shooting Wednesday afternoon, aren't we?"

"Yes, sir," Geordie said, and went out. As he walked toward his next class he thought rather unhappily about Catton. From what Catton had said, it had sounded as though he would be one of the party going to Laysan. The man had a nasty feel about him, something beyond Geordie's experience but disquieting; the narrowing of his eyes, for which there had been no reason because he didn't know Geordie, made the boy feel that Catton was full of an active hostility and maybe something more.

They decided to shoot the blind on Wednesday afternoon, and by the time they got there and were nicely settled the weather, which had been moderate for a few days, began to give signs of changing. Far to the northwest a dark bank of clouds began to roll up, and a cold wind began to blow. They didn't pay much attention to it, for small bunches of ducks began to come in and they were busy for awhile. Presently there was a lull in the flights, they sat down to get out of the wind, and Doc, who had been rather quiet all afternoon, cleared his throat.

"Meant to speak to you about the other day," he said. "I'm sorry about the way Catton acted."

"He didn't seem to like me very much," Geordie said.

"I don't think he likes anybody very much. He's a strange fellow, but some of his ornithological papers have been brilliant. Not that that makes it any easier to get along with him."

"Is he going to Laysan?"

"I'm afraid so," Doc said. "His university is putting up some of the money, and wants him to go along." He was silent for a long moment. "Geordie, are you going to be a naturalist, or a lawyer? I know it sounds like a silly question, for everything you do points in one direction. But I've talked with your Uncle Harry about this, and he tells me you're pulled both ways."

Geordie's face lit up with a big grin. "If you've talked to Uncle Harry you've thought of asking me to go," he said. "Oh, Doc, I want to more than . . ." He grew serious again as the import of Doc's question reached him. "I told you my father wanted me to be a lawyer. Maybe I ought to do what he says, but I want to be a naturalist. Doc . . . Doc, what should I do?"

Doc was looking at him, as he had once before, with an

abstracted, unfocused stare. Finally he shook his head, blinked, and his eyes focused again. "I'll take a chance," he said, as though to himself, and stuck his finger out. "I'm no wiser than anyone else," he said. "I try not to advise people, but I will go so far as to say this: I think the best thing, the happiest thing, is to do what you want to do. You'll have to work it out for yourself, but I'll help you if I can."

"Maybe Dad won't let me go," was all that Geordie said.

"Don't do anything about it," Doc said. "Leave it to Uncle Harry and me. And now that that's settled, let's get back to the business of the day." He stood up, moving out from under the roof of the blind. "Holy Christopher!" he exclaimed.

Geordie stood up quickly. It was snowing, the storm had moved in on them, and they had been so preoccupied that they hadn't noticed it. The flakes were coming down thickly, angled on the wind which had increased, and blotted out everything beyond a quarter of a mile or so. They had both experienced prairie blizzards a number of times, and were well aware of their dangers; the worst ones came up so swiftly and the snow was so blinding that farmers were sometimes caught between their houses and their barns and, unable to find their way, wandered about and froze to death.

They didn't waste time in talk and didn't take time to bring in the decoys. They gathered up their gear and their ducks and started for the shore. It had grown much colder suddenly and the water, which had been open in the main, was already beginning to grow slushy and thick and congeal around the bases of the reeds. A skim of ice was reaching out, and this slowed them. Doc almost lost his footing once, and if Geordie hadn't caught him would have gone down.

They reached the shore and with solid footing under them at last paused for a moment to get their breath, but they didn't stand long; the snow was thicker now and they quickly began to chill from the sweating they had done crossing the water. The wind whipped them and pushed them along; they were both grateful that they weren't facing it, or it and the snow would have blinded them. The going was bad enough without that for their horizon had closed in even more and was now down to a few yards. The storm had swallowed most of the afternoon light, and in the featureless grayness filled with snow they could see nothing; they could only keep the wind in the same quarter as it had been when they started.

It soon seemed to them that they had been walking for a long time, and they weren't sure where they were. In such a situation the mind stretches time out and begins to construct fears for itself. Could they possibly find the carriage, a tiny dot lost on the vast plain? They hadn't mentioned to anyone where they were going, but should they have stayed in the blind, where they had a little protection, and hope the storm would soon blow itself out? Had they been fools to leave, would they wander until they fell? They fought against these thoughts, and began to stumble occasionally. Presently they stopped, held up their ducks, nodded to each other and dropped the ducks. Then they clasped hands for reassurance.

Finally Geordie began to feel an uneasiness that was not connected with these thoughts in his mind; it strengthened and superimposed itself upon them. He didn't understand it at first; the storm battered at him and distracted him, but presently, as this uneasiness grew clearer, he realized that it was trying to tell him that their direction was wrong. It was a feeling, a sense of location, the mysterious sense that animals and a few people possess; somehow he had developed it over the

few impressionable years of his wanderings. It had guided him before, and now it was speaking to him again. He stopped and pulled Doc to a stop with him, and put his face close to Doc's.

"We're headed wrong!" he screamed above the wind, and pointed off almost at a right angle. "We ought to be going there!"

Doc stared at him. "Are you sure?" he screamed back. "The wind . . ."

"I think it's shifted! I *know* we ought to go that way!"

Doc stared at him a moment longer through the whirling snow, and then nodded. He could never say later why he had trusted Geordie's decision. "Thought had nothing to do with it," he would say. "I just knew in my guts that that kid somehow had it, that he was right."

Still holding hands, they turned and went on through the deepening snow. They were crossing the wind now, so the going was worse; they were blinded by the snow and the cold seemed to increase by the minute. Time drew out again and then, when hope began to fade into a numb, increasing weariness, they heard, upwind, the whinnying of the horse.

Neither of them thought at the moment that if their luck had taken them a few yards to the other side they couldn't have heard it for the wind; they stopped and hugged each other in gladness. Then they ran to the horse, took up the heavy hitching weight that had held it there, scooped out some of the snow that had blown in between the curtains of the carriage, climbed in, and gave the horse its head.

Wrapped in blankets in his bed, full of hot soup and with several hot water bags around him, Geordie hovered on the edge of sleep. His mother and father and

Doc, who was wrapped in a blanket and was staying for the night, stood looking down at him.

"Getting warm now?" his father asked.

"Yes, sir. I'm good and warm."

His mother leaned over and kissed him. "Good night, my darling. I'm so glad. Oh, I'm so glad."

Geordie put his arms around her neck and took her kiss, and she straightened up again, smiled at the men, and went out of the room. The two men looked at Geordie again. He had closed his eyes and his breathing had changed; he was already asleep.

"He got us to the carriage," Doc said. "I would never have found it. He's wonderfully at home in the out-of-doors."

"It seems a needlessly dangerous life, for small gain," Alfred Sutton said. "I will feel great relief when he finally decides to give it up."

"Would you let him go on an expedition with me?" Doc asked. "We usually take a student on these affairs, and I'd like very much to have Geordie."

"Indeed? Where does the expedition go?"

"Out to the Pacific," Doc said, "under the auspices of the Biological Survey."

"I appreciate your interest in Geordie," Alfred Sutton said, "but I am not at all sure that I would approve of his going so far. No reflection on you, of course."

Doc started to say something, and then decided not to. Alfred Sutton nodded to him, and went out of the room. Doc stood for a moment looking down at the boy, then reached out and stroked his forehead, very lightly, before turning out the light and leaving the room.

He left the next morning, before Geordie was awake, but the storm held for three days and increased in fury. If they had stayed in the blind, they would never have gotten out of it.

TWELVE

Several evenings later Doc stopped in at Uncle Harry's house and told him about the talk with Alfred Sutton. "I finally asked him the question directly," he said, "and he remarked that he doubted he'd approve Geordie's taking the trip. So, if you're still inclined for a bit of guerilla warfare, I suppose you'd better get started. There isn't too much time left."

"I've already gotten started," Uncle Harry said. "I thought he'd react that way. When did you get a chance to ask him?"

Doc had sketched in their homecoming, but had not

gone into any detail; now he did. "Geordie had already fallen asleep," he said, ending his story. "We were standing by his bed. Harry, there's no doubt the boy saved my life. I have a sense of obligation to him I'll never be able to fulfill. I'll break my neck to give him what he wants, and he wants to go. What is it you've done?"

Uncle Harry grinned. "I saw Moncrief, the warden, a few days ago and told him about our suspicions of Possum. He hid out in the marsh and caught Possum in the act, with a net. There's going to be a trial."

"I don't see—"

"I know you don't. You're too pure in heart, and too removed from the world in your ivory tower. To let you in on a grimy secret, I got Moncrief his job originally. I have my sticky little fingers in some of the politics hereabouts, although it's not generally evident. Moncrief knows exactly why I wanted Possum snared. I told him."

"You told him?" Doc asked, mystified. "What's that got to do with it?"

"At the right time, word will get around to Alfred that Geordie might be asked to testify about a former offense with dynamite."

Doc stared at his friend. "Glory be," he said finally. "I never suspected such depravity."

"I'll thank you to forget it."

"Yes," Doc said. "Indeed I will. But, you know, your maneuvers will have that boy in court, and the effect on him will . . ."

"Alfred won't have him in court. Alfred will have him safely out of the way. Probably as far out of the way as the middle of the Pacific Ocean," Uncle Harry said, and began to laugh at the expression on Doc's face.

The expression went from incredulity to a sort of outrage. "I don't believe it," Doc said finally. "Harry, you can't be serious. You're pulling my leg. Why, honest

men wouldn't allow, or couldn't live under such a . . .
 such a . . ." Words failed him.

"My friend," Uncle Harry said, "I accepted long ago a state of affairs that you couldn't admit to yourself. The world isn't run by honest men; it's run by schemers and rascals, and honest men do allow it."

Doc shook his head. "I'll never admit it," he said. "But be that as it may, all of this will come to nothing. Everything hinges on the date of the trial, and I doubt very much if you can arrange that."

"Don't be too sure," Uncle Harry said.

"What? Don't tell me that you got the judge his job too."

"No," Uncle Harry said. "But he's an old friend, we went to school together, and he'll do it as a favor to me. I did explain some of the circumstances to him."

Doc threw up his hands, and got to his feet. "I'd better go," he said. "I'm glad you left me a little faith in the judiciary."

Uncle Harry stood up and went with him to the hat-rack in the hall, and helped him on with his coat. "Remember," he said, "not a word of this to anybody."

"Have no fear," Doc said. "Have no fear, you backwoods Machiavelli. I won't admit to anybody that I know you."

Geordie spent a few nervous days wondering what, if anything, was going on and trying to appear as though there was nothing unusual in his life. His mother judged his somewhat preoccupied air to be the result of his narrow escape in the blizzard and cosseted him out of gratitude that he was still alive; his father, after a week during which he showed more than ordinary affection, became preoccupied himself. Geordie could put only one interpretation on this, and the tension within him increased. Everyone in the house, even Ingrid, seemed to be walking around on tiptoe and he felt like a conspirator. Being by nature a frank and open boy, he didn't like the feeling in the least and was out of the house as much as possible.

He spent a good deal of time with Dr. Black, learning as many sidelights as he could about the skinning of birds and the preparation of their skins; he soaked up all he heard about the needs of a diorama maker in the matter of observations on the spot, and built several model dioramas himself. This last pointed out to him a number of things he wouldn't have thought of: little details of botany, and effective and accurate arrangement that would also please the eye.

Dr. Black, ordinarily a somewhat remote and lonely man (he admitted once that he usually asked the world "Why? Why?" when he got up in the morning) took a liking to him, and they often chatted like old friends together. They didn't mention the expedition, although Geordie thought that Dr. Black must know about it because he worked pretty closely with Doc and they seemed to get on well together. Geordie wondered about this reticence and finally, one day when he asked Dr. Black if he knew Catton, received a clear indication that life wasn't any more a matter of sweetness, light, and selfless cooperation in the academic world than it was in any other.

"Catton?" Dr. Black asked, with a sidewise look at Geordie. "Yes, I know him."

"Dr. Satterthwaite said he didn't think Dr. Catton liked anybody."

"What brought out that observation?"

"He didn't seem to like me when I met him, and I

asked Doc about him. That's what Doc—Dr. Satterth-

waite—said."

"You can call Sat Doc to me, Geordie. We're all friends together. But you would be wise not to talk about one scientist to another, as a general rule. I regret to say that there are jealousies and a tendency toward backbiting in some of them. Dr. Catton is a powerful man in his field, and not always quite balanced when he thinks someone has crossed him. I sometimes wonder . . . But I had better take my own advice to you, and be discreet. Be careful if you have any relations with him. So much for that. You would be better employed looking for some chemical besides arsenic to use in treating skins than thinking about Catton. A number of good men have been killed when they grew careless in the use of arsenic. Never grow careless with it yourself."

"I try to remember every time I use it," Geordie said. "You told us about it when the class started, and that scared me enough to make me keep it in my mind." He grinned. "I guess I'd better go. Thank you for telling me."

Dr. Black smiled back at him and he went along to the Laysan diorama, to stand in front of it for a little while before he went home. He had been doing this occasionally for the last few days, for it was open to the public now and contemplation of it seemed to lessen the conspiratorial feeling within him. As he looked beyond the birds and the vegetation at the blue Pacific in the background, glistening white where the waves broke over the reef, he thought about the things he had heard of Catton and wondered what Dr. Black had been about to say and had decided not to. The words "not quite balanced" came back again, and Geordie wondered whether the unfinished phrase was to have been an extension of it, an even unhappier judgment. He suddenly felt a little chill run up his back, as though he feared that the adventure he had looked forward to for so long and had hoped for so ardently was going to be made difficult or even be spoiled by the man he had met in Doc's office.

Doc had said that Catton was hard to get along with, but Dr. Black had gone further and upset him—not only about Catton but about many other scientists as well. Geordie in his innocence had held scientists as a class to be above the self-serving maneuverings of other men, and now he knew that they, or at least some of them, were not. Perhaps, he thought, his father, who knew the world, had been thinking of this all the time. A feeling of his own inadequacy and naiveté confused and depressed him, and he turned away from the diorama and started home.

Dinner was a quiet meal. Geordie had little to say and his father was still preoccupied; Lavinia Sutton tried to lighten the atmosphere but finally fell silent too, and after dinner was finished went off to a bridal shower for a neighbor's daughter. As soon as the door had closed after her Alfred Sutton said: "I'd like to talk to you for a few minutes, Geordie."

"Yes, sir."

"Let's go into the library," Alfred Sutton said.

They went into the library and Ingrid brought the coffee service in. Alfred Sutton poured himself a cup. "Would you like some too?" he asked.

"No, sir, I guess I won't have any."

Alfred Sutton, standing by the coffee table, put sugar into his cup and stirred it. It was evident that he was having a difficult time getting around to what he wanted to say. He picked up his cup, set it down again, took a few steps around the room, and then sat down. "The night you and Dr. Satterthwaite got home in the blizzard, he said that he would like to take you on an expedition that he's making shortly. Apparently this is occasionally done with promising students, and he seemed to think that you are a promising one."

"Yes, sir."

"That, at least, was pleasant to hear." He took a sip of coffee. "You've heard something of this expedition, I take it."

"Yes, sir, a little. It's to Laysan Island."

"Yes." He took another sip of coffee. "I've talked with Dr. Satterthwaite a bit more about it. It seems to be for the shooting of rabbits and some birds that appear to be becoming extinct. I assume that it can be justified scientifically . . ."

He let the sentence hang in the air, as though to imply that while the enterprise made sense to the scientists it made little to him. Geordie didn't say anything. He had been growing increasingly tense as his father circled the point, and by now had great difficulty sitting still. In the afternoon, standing before the cyclorama, he had almost wished he had never heard of Laysan; now he wanted with all his heart to go. Alfred Sutton finished his coffee, carefully put the cup down, and looked at Geordie; Geordie slide forward a little in his chair and moved his feet to conceal the trembling of his knees.

"I must say," Alfred Sutton went on, "that I am astonished at the way these scientists seem able to get about, especially upon such errands as this one. There have been several expeditions to this rather obscure and deserted Island. One would have thought that everything possible has been learned about it. But perhaps I didn't quite understand, from what Dr. Satterthwaite told me, the importance of going there again."

"It's the rabbits," Geordie said desperately. "They . . ."

He swallowed and fell silent; a feeling that he and his father were trying to communicate in different languages descended upon him. He suddenly seemed to be running a temperature; the palms of his hands grew damp with perspiration, and his clothes stuck to him. He began to feel a little giddy and then he heard, as though from a distance, his father speaking again.

"However, I have decided to let you go," Alfred Sutton said, and for an instant looked as though he had bitten into something very unpleasant.

There was a short silence, for it took a moment for Geordie to comprehend what had been said, and then he found himself on his feet without knowing how he had gotten there. "Dad!" he said. He couldn't seem to say more; his emotions were too much for him. He opened and closed his mouth several times and then managed to say: "Thank you, Dad. Thank you very much."

Despite the fact that he had given his permission only because of circumstances that he han't been able to change, Alfred Sutton was moved too; he began to extend his hand to put it on Geordie's shoulder, but because his own emotions were confused, and because he had always disliked any show of emotion, he withdrew it. They stood for a moment looking at each other and then Geordie suddenly moved close to him, kissed him on the cheek, and turned and walked quickly out of the room and up the stairs.

THIRTEEN

The next morning Geordie hurried to Doc's office and forgot to knock before he pushed open the door. Doc was sitting surrounded with papers, and looked up. "I can go!" Geordie said. "My father's going to let me go!"

Doc stood up, and they shook hands. "Geordie, I'm delighted. I'll have a list for you in a day or two of the things you're to take. You and I will be leaving two weeks from tomorrow. We'll meet the rest of the crowd in San Francisco and go to Honolulu on an Army transport. You'd better go see Black." He smiled. "Oh," he said, and stuck his finger out. "You may be the camp cook, and have to deal with turtles, fish, and whatever supplies they give us that will last ten weeks or so without refrigeration. It might be a good thing to have a conference with that Ingrid, and make up a list of spices and whatnot that you'll need. It will be a long swim to the nearest store."

"If you think I can cook well enough."

"No false modesty. You're a master chef, my boy. I still remember that stew on the opening day. In fact, that's what got me interested in you—that and the fact that you skin birds well. You'll work like the deuce, poor fellow."

"I sure worried about that stew. I wanted you to be impressed."

"You were scheming even then?"

"Yes, sir."

"It seems to run in the family," Doc said obscurely. "Well, off you go. I'll see you later."

Geordie went along to see Dr. Black, whom he found skinning a beautifully marked snowy owl.

"Thought I'd better attend to it myself," Dr. Black said, straightening up and putting his scalpel down. "It's the handsomest one I've ever seen. Came from up around the northern end of the state somewhere. You look pleased with yourself this morning."

"I'm going to Laysan," Geordie said. "My father told me last night I could go."

Dr. Black solemnly shook hands with him. "Congratulations," he said. "May it be the first of a lifetime of expeditions. I had heard that this was in the wind, but I didn't want to speak prematurely. I think that I'll give you a copy of the order for materials that should meet you in San Francisco. You can double check Sat. If he doesn't lose his list, that is."

"Does he lose lists?" Geordie asked, surprised; Doc had always seemed very efficient.

"He gets carried away watching the wildlife, and forgets things. He lost a camera last time he was there. Maybe you'll find it again, ruined by the spray. I wish you'd sort of keep an eye on him."

"I will," Geordie said, pleased. Doc's talk about the cooking, bird skinning, spices to be taken and whatnot, combined with these new responsibilities, were already making him feel a member of the expedition and showing him that he had a real place in it. "Can I help you with the owl?"

"If you have a little time. I've worked out a tricky new cut to get out the skulls of birds with big heads, and you might find it useful."

Geordie took off his jacket and rolled up his sleeves, Dr. Black picked up his scalpel again, and they bent over the owl.

The next two weeks were so full of excitement and the activities of preparation that Geordie hadn't much time to think over his talk with his father, the remarks he had heard about Catton, or anything else not having to do directly with the expedition. Of all these matters the one concerned with his father was most often at the edge of his thought and sometimes, just before he fell asleep at night, he recalled his father moving a hand toward him and then withdrawing it and his own feeling that they had been talking in different languages. This brought a melancholy upon him as he dropped off to sleep and once or twice he had a recurrence of the dream in which his father moved further and further away and finally vanished; he would recall it momentarily the next day with a feeling of sadness tinged with guilt, but he was so excited and busy that these things were pushed into the back of his mind. Sooner or later the time would come when he would have to cope with them, but it was not upon him yet.

Doc had arranged for his absence, and he had conferences with his professors to lay out the studying he was to do while he was away. There was a good deal of studying to be done, and he was glad that Christmas vacation would shorten the class time that he would lose. He also spent hours with Ingrid and his mother, and his calculations as to probable meals and quantities, based upon various mysterious ingredients such as turtles and birds' eggs, was a liberal education in mathematics in itself.

"Maybe I ought to be able to make some cookies too," he said to Ingrid, at one point.

"Ja, cookies would please. I show you."

"I think one or two kinds would be enough," his mother said, "and you should only make them about once a week. If you let them, they'll have you making cookies every other day. If they can all eat cookies the way you can, you'll need another ship to carry the materials."

"Maybe we'll all have to go on a diet,' Geordie said, as Ingrid began to gather together the ingredients for the cookies.

"I do hope you will," Lavinia Sutton said. "Your Uncle Harry says that there won't be a doctor there, and I'll worry about your getting sick the whole time you're gone."

Laverty had come in with an armful of wood for the stove while she was saying this; he stood and listened until she had finished. "Ah, now, Ma'am," he said. "Don't be after worryin'. He's never had a sick day in his life, and he'll stand fine against the heathen microbes in those parts. A lad as could get home from that blizzard, a new ax couldn't kill him." He put the wood down, and turned to Geordie. "Maybe you could be bringin' me home one of those hula skirts."

"For yourself, Laverty?" Lavinia Sutton asked.

"Not for myself, Ma'am, savin' your presence. I was thinkin'," he said, sidling toward the door, "of givin' it to Ingrid to wear on Swedish Flag Day."

He disappeared; Ingrid turned quickly to the wall cabinets, pretending she hadn't heard him, but a dark blush crept up the back of her neck.

At first it had seemed to Geordie that the day of departure would never come, and then suddenly it was upon him. He had little appetite for breakfast; his stomach didn't seem to belong to him. He hadn't slept well and now, thinking of the vast distances that would separate him for the first time from everything that was familiar and the people that he had known all his life, he had a sort of queasiness. His mother smiled at him frequently but was rather silent; his father ate his breakfast methodically, pushed his chair back a little, and leaned forward.

"I won't be going to the depot with you, Geordie," he said, "but your mother and your Uncle Harry will be there. I hope you will make the most of the trip. I'm sure that your observations, both of the people and of the work itself, will bring you to a decision about your future. You are fortunate in being able to go and judge whether that way of life will give you the satisfaction, both mentally and materially, that you would find elsewhere. You know I would like you with me, in the law; you've heard my opinion that our world here is changing and that the law will have an increasingly important place in it." He came to a stop, and stood up; Geordie stood up too. They shook hands.

Geordie, already involved in the emotions of his impending departure, was so moved by his father's careful attempt at summing-up that he couldn't say anything; he gripped his father's hand hard, trying to express his gratitude and affection.

"Good luck, boy," Alfred Sutton said. "Be careful." This time he put his hand on Geordie's shoulder, squeezed it, and walked out of the dining room.

They heard him in the hall putting on his coat, and then they heard the closing of the front door as he left the house. Geordie, who had sat down again and bowed his head, raised it and looked at his mother. She was wiping her eyes, and she smiled tremulously at him.

"I'm sorry, Geordie," she said. "I didn't mean to cry, at least until you were gone. But he loves you very much, and he's so afraid of being emotional, and he wants so much for you to do what he thinks is best."

"I know, Ma," Geordie said.

She was about to say: "He's so often right, he's given people so much advice that's turned out to be correct, that we should listen to him." But she did not; she had seen the effect of Satterthwaite's lecture on Geordie and watched him since that evening; she knew how he loved the outdoors, and how onerous the dry and confining procedures of the law would be to him. Alfred Sutton had given them all a good life and she had vast respect for his intelligence, but her intuition told her that this time he might be wrong. She said: "We'll have to leave pretty soon. Had you better make a final check, and say good-by to Ingrid?"

"Yes, ma'am," Geordie said, and went off on his errands. The day took on a feeling of unreality. It seemed hardly any time before they were at the station, farewells were being said, and he was sitting by the window as the train gathered speed across the snowy world.

Doc went off somewhere and for awhile he sat alone,

staring out at the country he knew, still feeling the wrench of leaving and the pull of home. Then the country began to change and was new. It had no connection with his life, and this freed him. When Doc wandered back again and gave him a searching look, to know whether he was going to have a homesick boy on his hands for a time, Geordie said: "I guess we're really on our way at last, aren't we?"

"We are," Doc said. "We're really on our way."

FOURTEEN

The land gradually rose toward the backbone of the continent and continued to change. They came to the great wall of the Front Range, passed through it, and wound their way about westward through the mountains. Geordie was reminded of the two men with bobcat skins over their shoulders that he had seen so long ago on his trip with his father, and once more was moved by the peaks that thrust up into the sky, the shadowed canyons in which the white water streams were now covered with snow, and the snow-covered hanging forests of evergreens. They came out of the towering Wasatch Range into the deserts of the Great Basin, gradually left the snow behind for vast reaches of pale sand and pale, enduring vegetation and fantastically colored and jumbled rocks, and wound their way through snow again in the Sierra to descend into California's pleasant land.

Geordie was fascinated with it all; he was stuffed to bursting with impressions, and amazed by the variety and splendor of the part of America that he had seen. It seemed almost impossible to him that one country could be so vast and hold such differences, and when he considered that he had seen only a comparatively small segment it seemed more impossible still. The wonders of it made him want to see more, to move about and explore and know all of it; he didn't think he'd ever be satisfied until he did. He mentioned this to Doc as they neared San Francisco.

"It's a good start," Doc said. He had been enjoying Geordie's reactions. "But you'd better begin to think how to budget your time. There are half a dozen or so other continents that are going to need your attention sooner or later."

"You can kid me if you want," Geordie said, "but I'm going to try."

"If we weren't running so late because of the snow," Doc said, "I'd show you around San Francisco. Chinatown and all. But late as we are we'll have to get right to the ship, and it's too bad. They've done a great deal since the earthquake and the fire six years ago, and I can't think of a pleasanter town."

Geordie's impressions of San Francisco were hasty and confused, gathered between the railroad station and the ship: the white buildings and the steep hills, the busy waterfront and lovely bay. The ship had been waiting for them, and they were no sooner in their cabin and unpacking than there was a knock at the door and as it opened a ruddy, weathered face topped with close-cropped gray hair appeared. The man's eyes were bright blue, and his cheeks bunched up and almost hid them when he smiled. "Hi, Sat," he said. "I was about to log you as a deserter. Good to have you aboard."

"I'm glad we made it," Doc said. "We ran all the way." They shook hands. "This is Geordie Sutton. I wrote you about him. Captain Maguire, Geordie. You don't have to salute. Just call him Cap."

Maguire stepped into the room and clasped Geordie's hand. "Nice to meet you, Geordie. From what Sat says about you I think we'll get along fine."

Geordie liked him at once. "Yes, sir," he said. "I think we will." He stood aside, looking at the big man, and let Doc and Maguire talk. He had been in the Navy, commanding destroyers, and was now retired; the Biological Survey had asked him to head the expedition, and Doc had told Geordie that he was just the man to keep the peace if scientific squabbles threatened to disrupt it. There was nothing very formal about the arrangement, Doc had said, but somebody had to be the final arbiter, and Maguire had been acceptable to everyone.

"Is Catton on board?" Doc asked.

"Been here for two days, but nobody's seen much of him. He gave me a hand the first morning he was here checking over the supplies. I haven't seen him since, but I take it he's here. We sail right after lunch. I'll let you finish unpacking, and see you at lunchtime."

He waved a hand and went out, and they finished stowing their clothes. Geordie pushed his bags under the lower bunk and straightened up. He hadn't thought of Catton for a time, but now that Catton's name had been mentioned the man was in his mind again, a sort of uncomfortable shadow. Geordie didn't want him there and was a little irritated at his own reaction, for he had seen Catton only once and it wasn't his habit to take such quick dislikes to anyone. He stood trying to puzzle it out, for his feeling was really more than a dislike; it was a sort of defensive hostility, and he had no reason to be hostile. He knew other people with bad manners, and didn't feel hostile toward them; he merely avoided them and thought no more about it.

"You look unhappy," Doc said, breaking in on his thought. "Something bothering you?"

Geordie decided not to go into it. "No, sir."

"Let's go take a walk around the ship."

"All right," Geordie said, glad to be distracted. "I'd like to. I've never been on a ship before."

They went on deck and wandered about until lunch was announced. They ate with the officers, and Catton wasn't there; Geordie said little, and listened to the others talk. Their talk was mostly of the sea and since many of their terms and references were unfamiliar to him he felt a little lost. Before lunch was finished there was a bustle that indicated they were getting under way, and Geordie excused himself and went out on deck to watch.

The lines were cast off and the ship began to tremble as her engines increased their revolutions; a widening strip of water appeared between her and the wharf. The whistle's bellow made Geordie jump; the bow swung, the engines settled to their working rhythm, and the ship gathered speed down the bay. The city, climbing its hills and pale in the sun, diminished astern and the ship began to rise and fall a little; Geordie, feeling really severed from the land for the first time in his life, was at once excited by the new experience and a little homesick for all the things he had always known and had learned how to cope with. Now everything was new and strange except the gulls riding the freshening breeze. As they approached the Golden Gate the motion of the ship increased, and after they had passed through it increased still more. An alarming queasiness moved in upon Geordie, and burgeoned into a dolorous nausea; his vision grew confused, and so did his sense of balance. His stomach turned traitor and cast up his lunch and finally, sweating, racked by his heaving interior, shamed and spastic, he clawed and staggered his way to his stateroom and hoped he would die.

It was two days before the sea flattened out and he lifted his head. Having always been healthy and untroubled by any ailments except very minor ones he wondered how he had survived such a fearful visitation, and was almost afraid to get out of bed lest he be smitten again. He felt drained and hollow as a drum, and a little light in the head. He watched the sunlight falling through the porthole for a time, wondering whether he dared to get up, and Doc came in.

"Well," Doc said. "You pulled through. I'm glad to see it. They were taking bets at the officers' table on the day of your demise."

Geordie smiled weakly. "I didn't think I'd make it," he said. "I remember you came in once in a while and held my head and covered me up. I sure felt awful. Does everybody get as sick as that?"

"One time or another. You'll probably be all right from now on. Are you going to join the human race again?"

"Do you think it would be all right?"

"I think so. I'll wait on the bow for you."

He went out, and Geordie got out of bed, dressed, and went up on deck. He was still a little light-headed, but when he came out on the foredeck into the sun he began to feel better. He walked to the bow, which was gently rising and falling, and joined Doc. The sharp stem parted the waves and turned up a bow-wave of gleaming white water; the Pacific stretched away limitless and calm. The salty air was just cool enough to be invigorating, and after a few deep breaths Geordie felt himself again. The homesickness that had descended upon him in the bay was gone, and at last he began to enjoy himself.

After a time Doc went off to talk to Maguire, and a little later a few porpoises appeared and played alongside the bow, keeping pace with the ship. Their maneuvers were so fluid and graceful, so plainly arising from a spirit of joyful play, that Geordie lost himself in watching them until Doc came back and tapped him on the shoulder.

"Time to eat," Doc said. "You must be ready."

Geordie turned reluctantly from the porpoises, and realized that he had never been so hungry in his life. "I guess I'm about starved to death," he said, "but the porpoises are so pretty I hate to leave them."

"You're really just beginning to live. It will be even better when we get to the island, but you'll miss it if you die now from starvation. Come along."

Aside from a storm that night the weather remained clear and tranquil, and now that Geordie had his sea legs he had a wonderful time. Catton, whom Geordie gathered was always sick when he was on the sea, stayed in his cabin; Doc and Cap were often conferring together, and Geordie was left more or less to his own devices. This suited him very well. He was all over the ship and made friends with everybody; he was usually on deck when the sun came up, and stayed there most of the day; he discovered flying fish and sharks, Leach's petrels, and had his first sight of black-footed albatrosses. Three of these great wanderers of the trackless ocean, with their seven foot wing-spread, appeared at dawn in the wake of the ship and showed him their consummate mastery of the air as they hovered and lifted and slid along the wavecrests on motionless wings. They had had a special significance ever since he had first read *The Rime Of The Ancient Mariner* in school, and he knew there were thousands of them on Laysan; he had read up on them in the University library. They were romantic birds to him, at home on the vast reaches of the western ocean; there were usually a few of them in sight for the rest of the trip, and he never tired of watching them.

The ship steamed on. Several days later they sighted the island of Molokai at sunset, and the next morning drew in under Diamond Head. A cloud clung to the crest, and the ancient, extinct volcanoes of Oahu, rising massively from the sea, were clothed in mossy green. The ship docked and old friends of Doc's and Maguire's greeted them with leis. Honolulu was a small town, easy-going and friendly in the soft, warm air, and among the palm trees and flowers, the bright colors and strange mixture of people, Geordie felt a long way from the snowy prairies where winter would hold the land for a long time yet.

It was all so different from the little college town that he had left he might have been a little homesick if he'd had time, but Cap wanted to get all their arrangements completed now that he was ashore. "If Geordie and I take our bags to the hotel and come back here to check the supplies as they're unloaded and moved over to the KITTIWAKE," he said to Doc, "you can wait for Catton to come ashore. You have to take charge of the feathers they took from the Japs two years ago and see that they're burned, and we might as well get that done." He shook

his head. "They tell me they have eleven wagonloads. Those pirates must have killed a quarter of a million birds. We'll see you at the hotel about dinner time."

He and Geordie left with the bags, returned, and spent most of the afternoon checking their supplies as they were brought to the revenue cutter which would take them to Laysan. It was dirty work, and after they had finished they went for a swim. It was Geordie's first swim in salt water, and its buoyancy and the way the waves carried him up delighted him. They visited Doc's friends in the evening; the next day they saw a little of the island from a carriage, swam again in the clear water, went to the Aquarium, and were on KITTIWAKE by four o'clock.

At five the cutter cleared for Laysan, eight hundred miles to the northwest. She would pass many islands and shoals along the way, parts of the Leeward Islands chain that begin at Hawaii and extend to Midway and Ocean Islands at the end of the chain. They are the tops of an ancient volcanic mountain range that had been worn down by wind and weather and the sea and built upon by coral animals, older than the Hawaiian Islands and more eroded; most of them are surrounded by coral reefs and some of them are flat and stand only a few feet above the waves. They are lonely and remote, and only one of them, Necker Island, shows evidence of having been visited by Polynesian seafarers although they must have all been landed upon by these people at one time or another. Their very remoteness was what attracted the great legion of far-ranging seabirds to them to nest, for on them the birds were in large measure let alone.

KITTIWAKE would pause at several of them—Meeker Island, where the surf would be too rough for them to get ashore, and French Frigate Shoals, a few sand islands overshadowed by a precipitous rock whose pinnacle resembled a sailing ship. They would land on the sand island nearest the rock, but not stay very long because there were so few birds nesting.

FIFTEEN

They raised Laysan Island in the early afternoon, six days after leaving Honolulu, and as they closed it the air above the Island and the sea was full of birds. The deep blue water shaded off into pale green and aquamarine as it shoaled; a wind had come up within the last hour and the sea was very rough. The tall combers were breaking high and white, with long veils of wind-driven spray, on the reef and coral ledges and ochre-colored beach. Geordie, clinging to the rail between Doc and Cap, stared at the place that had been in his mind for so long. It had occupied his dreams and hopes and many of his waking hours, and now it was a reality. A red-tailed tropic bird, exotic and beautiful in its burnished plumage of pinkish white feathers, with a long tail that was red too, flying swiftly past close to the ship, seemed somehow in his mind to personify it.

The island was about two miles long and a mile wide, shaped like a bowl, and rose a little toward the center beyond the gleaming beach. Scanty underbrush covered the rising ground, and KITTIWAKE didn't rise high enough on the waves for him to see the lagoon that he knew was in the center. As they had approached it from the west after a wide half circle, he could see, small in the distance, the cottage where they would live, with two coconut palms in front of it and a hau tree on the side—the only trees on the island—the warehouses and the tower that had once been used as a lighthouse. The buildings had been constructed by the company that had taken the guano from the island years before. The ship was too far offshore to make out the birds on the beach, but there were great numbers of them in the air.

"The rabbits have eaten a lot more of it since I was here," Doc said gloomily. "It's beginning to look like a desert now."

A sailor came up and spoke to Cap and went off again. "Too late and too rough to land tonight," Cap said. "We're going to stand off and cruise a little until the morning. They don't want to chance dragging an anchor."

Geordie was itching to get ashore, but composed himself to wait; he knew that they would have to get through a passage in the coral in a lifeboat, and saw that they couldn't do it now. The wild water would swamp any boat without room to maneuver between the sharp coral heads, and no one could swim in such a place.

They stood by the rail until the island diminished astern, and went down to supper. They hadn't talked very much about the rabbits before, but now that they were about to land the animals were the main subject of their conversation. Doc was feeling depressed because of the changes that had taken place since he had been on Laysan before; even from the ship this change had been apparent.

"Doing away with the rabbits has got to be a holy crusade," he said, "and if anybody feels qualms about it I'll personally feed him to the frigate birds, in little pieces. We're not here to be sporting, we're here to undo a foolish act if we can, and it will be killing pure and simple, just like killing bacteria in an infected man. I don't know whether we got here in time to undo the damage or not."

"We'll know better tomorrow," Cap said, "and as soon as we get settled we'll get the rifles out. They'd better be carried at all times, everywhere we go."

"I think so too," Doc said. "The first month will be the most important. The rabbits will begin to get wary after awhile, and we'd better get as many as we can before that happens."

"What if they do get wary?" Cap asked. "Where will they hide? From what I could see this afternoon there aren't many places."

"The shearwaters and petrels dig burrows to lay their eggs in," Doc said, "and the rabbits will hide in them."

"Birds dig burrows? Come, now."

"They sure do," Doc said. "The shearwaters won't be nesting until May or thereabouts, but there will be petrels until Hades itself wouldn't hold 'em. You wait and see."

"I'll wait," Cap said. "Now I'm going to bed."

"Me too," Doc said. "We'll have to bestir ourselves tomorrow to get the stuff ashore and get settled. Going to turn in, Geordie?"

"I think I will. Pretty soon. Good night."

The two men said good night in return, and went to their cabins. Geordie went out on deck, found a dark corner out of the wind, and got his back into it to look at the stars for a little while. The ship rose and fell lazily, for a good deal of the wind had gone down with the sun. As his eyes grew accustomed to the darkness he began to see pale, flitting, dove-sized forms occasionally as they sped through the few bands of light from the ship. They looked like little ghosts and puzzled him for a short time until two of them dodged past making strange little squealing sounds, and then he remembered from his reading that petrels make such sounds and are nocturnal, hiding in their burrows by day and flying about at night. One of them startled him badly by suddenly appearing out of the darkness and hovering before his face with a thrumming of wings and sounds like a growling kitten; he threw both hands up and it slid off, leaving him to compose himself and finally laugh a little at his fright.

Even more than the tropic birds and the distant albatrosses he had seen in the afternoon it seemed a strange small spirit of the place where tomorrow he would go ashore into a remote little world that would be so different from the one he knew. A small shiver of anticipation went up his back and he had a moment of gratitude that he, of all the people in the world, was fortunate enough to have this adventure. Then he went off to bed.

They had anchored off the island when Doc awoke him, and he could hear the bustle of activity on deck. He dressed quickly, went to the salon and swallowed a hasty breakfast, and joined the others on deck. There was a cloud of birds over Laysan; the lifeboat was loaded for the first trip and the sailors were climbing in and taking their places at the oars, and at Doc's gesture he went over the side and got into the bow of the boat. Catton, looking pale and gaunt, came to the rail and was helped in next; he took a seat in the middle of the boat and stared unhappily at the floorboards, and Doc and Cap got aboard. The rest of the crew gathered on deck waved to them and they shoved off and the sailors bent to the oars.

It was a calm and pleasant ride until they got to the narrow opening in the reef, and then the boat began to pitch and there was white water all around them; Geordie thought several times that they would be capsized before they got through. He was kept busy hanging on, and they were all soaked with spray before they rode a wave in and grounded on the beach. Geordie jumped out and was the first ashore, which pleased him; he almost fell down before he adjusted to being on the solid earth again. The boat was pulled up a little higher on the beach and they began to unload it. Catton staggered a few yards higher on the beach, sat down, and was sick for the last time; Geordie had the grace to feel sorry for him.

When the boat was unloaded the sailors took it out again through the surf for another load, and for a moment Geordie stood and watched them, full of admiration for their skill, and then took his first look about. There was an air of decline, almost of barrenness about what he could see, for the grass was thin and patchy and the few low, scraggly bushes seemed to be dying, but he was too excited to notice it at first because it was so full of life. The beach, far to the north and south, was dotted with a multitude of big, dusky, black-footed albatrosses, as big as geese, wandering about, groaning, quacking, or screeching at each other, clapping their bills, or asleep; occasionally one would come in from the sea and land clumsily, sometimes pitching forward and falling over itself, and the birds that took off made long runs to get airborne. Many of them watched the men but showed no fear or apprehension; it was a little unsettling to see birds so tame and unconcerned. Gulls, terns, a few red-footed boobies, white Laysan albatrosses with dark backs and wings, and great frigate birds were in the air. Big birds were everywhere, wild birds that paid no attention to people; it was an astonishing and almost unbelievable sight. Of the terns the gray-backs were the most numerous and the noisiest; pretty and graceful, they swooped down on the people until they were almost head height before they swerved off.

Doc, who had been looking around too, turned to Geordie. "Quite a few birds left, huh?" he shouted, above the din.

"You told me, but I didn't imagine it would be like this," Geordie shouted back. "It's wonderful! All the birds of the ocean must be here!"

"This is only part of them. Let's begin to get the stuff carried up. They'll have another load in soon."

They picked up as much as they could carry and began to climb up the beach toward the buildings. Cap picked up a load and followed them. As they got into the thin grass and the portulaca they began to see rabbits, which seemed to be everywhere. The buildings, when they came to them, were lined along the foundations with rabbit holes, and rabbits were hopping about the thin, scattered grass around them. There was a honey eater, a little smaller than a robin and a brilliant vermilion in color, perched on a twig of the hau tree beside the house, and when it saw them it began to sing. Its song, so different from the raucous uproar of the sea birds, seemed like a welcome, and because of this the honey eaters were Geordie's favorite birds as long as he was on the island.

They stood for a moment smiling at it, and then dropped their loads and went into the cottage but didn't get much further than the door. The Japanese feather hunters who had raided the island two years before had lived in it and left it incredibly filthy, and the three of them spent the next hour cleaning out the worst of the trash. They left the door open and raised the windows to get the sea air through, and the honey eater which had welcomed them came in and hunted moths while they worked.

After they had gotten the cottage into fairly livable condition they turned to the cistern, which they intended to use to catch rainwater from the roof, and found that it was unusable. It was filled with the dessicated bodies of birds, for after cutting off their wings the Japanese had thrown them into the cistern; as they starved, and their body fat was used up, their skins didn't require cleaning. When KITTIWAKE, on patrol, had appeared and caught the raiders, the sailors hadn't thought to look into the cistern. Cap and Doc were dismayed at this discovery, for rain would be their only source of fresh water and they would have to find something else to store it in. They went to search about in the decaying warehouses. The first one, with one side blown away, held several thousand albatross wings; the next one had an old bathtub in it, and they cleaned this up and dragged it out under the eaves of the cottage where it would catch the rain.

Catton and several sailors came up with another load and they joined them on the return trip and spent the next several hours getting up their supplies from the beach. The rest of the day was spent in finishing the cleaning up of the cottage and getting their gear inside and arranged and fixing up the soundest of the warehouses as their workshop. Geordie set up the Army stove in a small building behind the cottage, stacked his supplies, and began to think about dinner. Cap and Doc came in with armloads of wood.

"We drew straws," Doc said. "We're the woodgatherers, and John is the dishwasher. I don't think he likes that very much, but it was an honest election. He won't have to wash any dishes tonight, for we haven't any water. I hope it rains. We've been working like the devil all day, so let's take a breather and a look at the estate."

Geordie had thought of climbing the tower for a view of the entire island when he had time and suggested that they do it, but when they got to the tower it was in such bad condition that they decided it would be too dangerous to climb. They spent a few minutes beside the cottage, looking west over the sea. There were dark clouds gathering far out, catching the rays of the declining sun around their edges, and holding the hope of a shower during the night; there were many birds in the air, and for a time the men were so engrossed in the view and their own thoughts that no one noticed that more rabbits seemed to be moving about now that evening was approaching.

Suddenly Cap snapped his fingers. "Rabbits!" he said. "I thought we came to shoot rabbits. Now's as good a time as any to start the crusade."

They went into the cottage and got rifles and several boxes of ammunition apiece, spread out in a line, and walked toward the southeast corner of the island. There were plenty of targets, and soon the rifles began to pop. As Doc had said, there was nothing sporting about it; yet if anyone had felt a distaste for this sort of execution it was soon dispelled by the melancholy state of the vegetation. They killed forty-five rabbits by the time the light grew so dim that they couldn't see their sights.

"Well," Cap said, as they walked back through the

twilight, "we've made a start, but it's a grimy sort of

business."

"Grimy indeed," Doc said. "No fun at all. But unless we keep at it the place will be a desert pretty soon. I wish that Company manager had let well enough alone. As I read the notes of people who were here about ten years ago, this was a green and beautiful place. The damage has accelerated even since I was here last year."

Geordie walked quietly along with them, trying to picture in his mind Laysan as it used to be. The introduction of the rabbits had been an ignorant and wasteful business; for the rabbits, unless controlled, would eventually all starve, and in the destruction they had brought about exterminate several species of birds which existed nowhere else in the world.

They could see the first light go on in the cottage as Catton lit a lantern. "You're pretty quiet, Geordie," Doc said.

"I was thinking how stupid it was," Geordie said, "bringing in the rabbits."

"So you're a little depressed too," Cap said, "like I am. We weren't brought up to do this kind of shooting, although intellectually we know it has to be done. Well, we'll have to adjust to it, and quickly."

"If you recall, I tried to get around to this last night on the ship," Doc said.

"I remember," Geordie said, "but it didn't sink in then. It has now."

They had reached the cottage by this time, and went in and put the rifles away. Catton was lighting another lantern and paused to say: "Heard you shooting. How many?"

"Forty-five, I think," Doc said.

"I got fifteen. Pretty good start for the craziest rabbit hunt in history." He looked at Geordie. "When do the heroes eat?"

"Pretty soon," Geordie said. He lit his own lantern, and went out the door. He was thinking of Catton's look, which had been sardonic and seemed to imply that he didn't believe Geordie could cook anything fit to eat, but Geordie forgot this as he went around the corner of the house for there was a sound in the air like a wind blowing through trees. He stopped, puzzled, and suddenly there was a white-breasted petrel in front of his face that startled him as badly as the one on the ship had startled him. He ducked aside and the bird vanished; he turned the lantern up and saw many ghostly bodies flitting by. It was their crying that made the sound; there seemed to be hundreds of them. He ran around to his cookhouse and went inside and closed the door, for they gave him an eerie feeling and at the moment he wanted to get away from them. He started his fire, opened cans, and went to work. He was so busy that he didn't see another petrel fly in through the open window; as he stood stirring the stew in the saucepan it landed on his shoulder and he jumped as though he had been stung.

It left his shoulder but was soon back again, and he caught it gently, put it out the door, took off his shirt, and hung it over the window to keep any others out. He wanted to start off with a tasty meal, and the birds were too distracting. When he took the dinner around to the cottage door the moaning cries of the petrels were still going on, and he found the door shut and the windows curtained to keep them out.

"We didn't mean to exclude you," Doc said, as he backed in the door, "but this place was filling up with visitors."

"I know," Geordie said, "one tried to sit on my shoulder while I cooked, and I'm not used to birds in the kitchen. I'll be back as soon as I get my shirt."

When he returned they were eating enthusiastically, but paused long enough for comment.

"Now they believe me," Doc said.

"Sat made no mistake," Cap said. "If this is a fair sample, I'll stay."

Catton gave Geordie a sidewise look. "Not bad," he said grudgingly. "Not bad."

Geordie looked back at them, and decided he could afford a comment of his own. "It's just because you're so hungry," he said innocently. "You were seasick for so long."

The other two men bowed their heads to hide sudden smiles; Catton gave Geordie an inimical stare and began eating again. After a short silence conversation picked up again, but he didn't join it and left the table as soon as he was finished. Geordie wasn't pleased with his small triumph for very long; he soon began to wonder why he had gone out of his way to begin making an enemy when Catton's churlishness wasn't sufficient reason for it. Either Cap or Doc, in a like circumstance, would have laughed and acknowledged they'd got the worst of it; Catton seemed to take it as an insult and withdrew to nurse his grievance.

It had been an odd day. Catton was a puzzle. Geordie pushed his chair back, and as he did so the door blew open and a petrel walked in, climbed up his leg, clawed its way to his shoulder, and sat there calmly looking about.

It was a sleek and pretty bird about a foot long, with tubed nostrils, gray on the back, black on the nape, wings, and tail, with a white belly and forehead. Its tameness and unconcern in the midst of people were extraordinary.

Doc got up and shut the door. "Don't look so flabbergasted," he said to Geordie. "You'll get used to it."

SIXTEEN

The storm moved in and it rained most of the night; the bathtub was full in the morning and their water problems were taken care of for the time. Geordie was up early and watched the sun rise over the sea, making a bright path over the dark water and faintly coloring the spray on the reef. It looked as though they were going to have a beautiful day, and he hoped to be able to explore the island after the morning's work was done. Just as he was about to move off toward the kitchen a snow-white fairy tern, the most beautiful of sea birds, came in from the sea and hovered over him for a moment, so close that he could see its large dark eyes; it looked almost ethereal

against the clear sky.

It flew off toward the south beach and he went into the house for a rifle before going to the kitchen, and while waiting for the fire to settle down walked behind the cookhouse and shot six rabbits. He was glad to find that he had somehow made the adjustment to such cold-blooded killing during the night, and wasn't depressed by it any more.

When he brought breakfast in there were half a dozen birds in the cottage—not petrels, which went back into their burrows when day came, but two miller birds, two Laysan finches, the honey eater, and the little gray-brown miller birds were flitting about after insects; the rail, a little pale olive-buff bird spotted with sienna and faint lilac gray, whose race had long since lost the ability to fly, was running about on the floor. None of them was paying the slightest attention to the people and as Geordie paused to look at them, seeing at one time four of the five birds that lived nowhere else in the world, one of the miller birds landed on Doc's head and sang its pretty song.

Geordie was enthralled by them; he stood holding his tray until the miller bird finished its song and took to the air again. "It's sort of like the Garden of Eden," he said. "It's a wonderful way to start the day."

"They've discovered us," Doc said. "They'll be here all the time now."

Geordie smiled with pleasure and put the tray down, and they fell to breakfast with the birds flitting about them. Cap announced the schedule for the day, and after breakfast was finished Catton went off with bad grace to wash the dishes and the rest of them went to work to finish the cleaning up of the house and the yard. Catton joined them after a time and they spent the rest of the morning planting young coconut and eucalyptus trees that KITTIWAKE had left for them, putting wire around them to keep off the rabbits. They all had rifles with them, and more rabbits were shot as they worked. Presently Cap called them together.

"The Indians," he said, "put in fish with their corn when they planted it, so we can bury a rabbit or two under every little tree."

"Sort of poetic justice," Doc said. "They cut all the young trees down, now they can help push them up again. It will help with the sanitary problem, too. What are we going to do with them when the trees are all planted? We can't have hundreds of dead rabbits lying around."

"We'll still have to bury them, or throw them into the sea. Well, back to work."

They spread out again and shot and dug until lunch time, which by common consent was a pick-up meal, and then they rested awhile. Catton took the shotgun and went off to do some collecting; the rest of them sat for a time, loaded the cameras, and then went for a swim. The water was clear and refreshing; it was Geordie's second exposure to salt water, and he was even more delighted than he had been in Honolulu by its buoyancy and the pleasure of contending with the waves and being carried effortlessly up on their soaring crests to see the island's whole western shore and the congregation of gonies (for he had already picked up this term for the albatrosses from Doc) on the beach and in the air. Doc had said something about exploring after lunch, but even with that prospect before him he hated to end his swim.

Cap and Doc finally closed in upon him and chased him out; they went up to the cottage, dressed, collected the rifles and cameras, and set out. Cap decided to go up the western shore; Doc and Geordie started south along the beach among the black-footed albatrosses—black gonies—that were scattered about. It was still strange to Geordie to have birds calmly move off only a few steps and watch him go by. Many of them didn't move at all. One that they stopped in front of had apparently just laid its egg, and when they stooped before it the bird got up, bent over, and touched the egg with its beak as though to point with pride to what it had accomplished.

They took pictures of it and went on to the little fresh-water pond in the island's southwest corner. There was bunch grass in this vicinity and a few Laysan rails were running about in it; two ducks, dusky, with dark faces and white patches around their eyes, were swimming in the middle of the pond. They didn't fly and only moved a little further toward the far shore.

"They're awfully tame," Geordie said, and then recognized them. "They're Laysan teal! Now I've seen all five species of Laysan's birds! Doc, do you think that these are all that's left of them? They can't be down to two."

"I certainly hope not. There were less than a hundred when I was here before, and we were worried then. Even at that, they were the rarest duck in the world. But only two . . . I can't believe it. You'd better make a project of getting here frequently to see if you can see more."

"Yes, sir."

"John was intending to collect a pair or two, but I'll have to call him off that. We have a few skins back home, and we'll give him a couple of those."

"Last night, when I said something about his being seasick all the time he didn't like it. I guess I shouldn't have said it."

"You were certainly within your rights," Doc said, "but as closely associated as we are, and will be for six weeks or so, I think you'd better go easy with him. He was always a difficult fellow, and seemed to think he was better than anyone else and up on a little pedestal, but this time he's worse than usual. I don't think he's well, and being shaken up on the trip and not eating enough to keep a snake alive hasn't been good for him. Be patient, and offer to help him if the chance comes up. You'll probably be rebuffed, but just let it go."

"I'm sorry I talked back to him."

"Don't be sorry. Think no more about it."

They started to walk again, and came out on the wide south beach. The gray-backed terns were preparing to nest there soon, and there were legions of them; presently there would be more coming in from the sea. They swooped and dove at Doc and Geordie, tame and noisy; there were one or two pretty fairy terns among them, for they also liked that beach, and the two men moved through them as through a playful, living storm. A little further to the east, where the number of terns thinned out and the offshore reef ended, they came upon a sea turtle that must have weighed three hundred pounds. They hauled it out on the beach and grunted and heaved until they had turned it over on its back, where it lay waving its flippers.

"We'll come back later and collect some steaks," Doc said. "The tide's going out, and the old girl won't be able to get on her feet until it comes in again." He pointed north, up the beach. "There will be a lot of black gonies up there, but let's cut over to the lagoon now."

They started up the little rise behind the beach and as they got into the thin vegetation and scattered low scaevola brush they began to run into rabbits again. They were everywhere, seemingly as thick on the ground as the birds were in the air, and Doc and Geordie shot until their guns were almost too hot to hold and they had to stop for awhile.

A few more steps took them high enough to see the

lagoon. They were above the southeastern end of it; it was nearly two-thirds as long and a quarter as wide as the island. There was a wide portulaca flat on the western side, where great numbers of Laysan albatrosses, gleaming white with black wings were nested, for they liked the protected location; frigate birds were gathered about in what was left of the dying brush along the eastern side.

"They're not nest-building yet," Doc said. "But they'll start next month."

He had hardly finished speaking when there were protesting squawks from above and behind them, and they turned to see a big white bird with black-edged wings coming in from the sea with a frigate bird after it.

"Masked booby," Doc said. "Watch this."

The squawking booby was dodging about among the other birds in the air trying to evade the pursuer, but it couldn't fly fast enough; the frigate bird, as beautiful a flier as Geordie had ever seen, flew rings around it, headed it at every turn, and finally caught it by the tail with its beak and upended it. The booby disgorged several fish, and the frigate bird dove, picked them out of the air before they reached the ground, and flew off with them. Geordie had to laugh at the booby's disconsolate squawks as it turned out to sea again.

"Poor booby," he said. "That was a dirty trick."

"That's probably why they're called boobies," Doc said. "They let the frigates work them half to death and never fight back. Let's go show the frigates they aren't the lords of creation that they get to thinking they are."

They walked over to the low scaevola brush where the frigate birds were gathered. They were big and dark, with long, strongly hooked beaks. After watching the attack on the booby Geordie wasn't sure he wanted to get very close to them, but they were calm enough. Several of them had such large crops that they couldn't fly even if they'd wanted to, and Doc picked up a long stick from the ground and tapped one of them smartly with it. The bird opened its beak, disgorged its fish, spread its great seven-foot wings and got into the air.

"See," Doc said. "The fish are as good as new. Flying fish. Any time we want a fish dinner, that's one way to get it. I hope that was the bird that robbed the booby."

Geordie examined the fish and found them perfectly fresh, for they hadn't started to be digested yet; they were held in the crop and passed one by one as the stomach made room for them. "I'd like to try a couple," he said, and strung two of them on a stick to carry along.

They shot more rabbits, and then went around to the other side of the lagoon. The Laysan albatrosses, white gonies, were all over the portulaca flats, for they liked the locality, and rails were running around; the sandy margin of the lagoon was occupied by turnstones and plover, bristle-thighed curlew and red phalaropes, and the air all around was full of winged creatures. Their variety and numbers were an amazing thing to see, and Geordie was fascinated by it.

"I thought I'd never see so many birds as I saw when we landed," he said, "but that wasn't anything compared to this."

"Too many to see at once. You can spend a lot of time here, and get to know them one by one. Let's go on north and see if we can find Cap."

They started out, weaving a wandering course between the gonies, and Geordie got into an area where the portulaca was a little thinner and suddenly went into the ground up to his hips. He was on the edge of the nesting territory of the petrels and the sandy ground was honeycombed with their burrows; he was so busy looking all around that he hadn't noticed it. Doc stood and laughed at his struggles to get onto firm ground again, for every time he got one foot on apparently solid earth he broke through again. Several petrels clawed their way out of

their demolished tunnels with him, and after a good deal
 of dusty rolling about he got back onto solid footing and watched where he was going thereafter.

"So that's where they go in the daytime," he said, when he got his breath back. "They've scared me at night, but I didn't expect they'd try to bury me during the day."

"You'll fall into their burrows once in awhile," Doc said. "Everybody does. You can't always be sure where they are, and you'll have your mind on something else and down you'll go. They'll start to lay pretty soon and be quieter at night, and then the shearwaters will get here and make even more noise. I must admit that birds that live in holes during the day and raise the devil at night seem very queer to me. I can't get used to it."

They went on, shooting rabbits along the way, and finally found Cap on the island's highest point near the northern beach. It was only about twenty-five feet high, but it gave a fine view over the sea where the surf was the most beautiful; Cap was sitting pensively on top of the little hill watching it, and started when they joined him.

"I had gotten to feeling that I was the only man here," he said. "Robinson Crusoe facing the empty sea. Ships practically never come this way. I doubt we'll see one while we're here, except KITTIWAKE when she stops back."

Geordie didn't know that KITTIWAKE was coming back. "She's coming here? he asked. "I thought she went home."

"She was going to Midway to have a look, and she'll stop in on her way back to Honolulu. But she won't stay more than an hour or so. After that we'll be marooned. Want to go home on her?"

"No, sir," Geordie said. "I like being marooned here."

"We might as well start back," Doc said. "We've got a

turtle turned over on the east side, and it will take a while to butcher it. Have you seen John?"

"He went by here an hour or two ago. I guess he's gone back to skin his bird."

As they started out Doc said: "Do you think we'd better ask him if he feels well enough to stay? I was saying to Geordie awhile ago that he didn't seem very well."

"He'd take it as a criticism," Cap said. "He doesn't seem well to me either, but maybe it was the trip. Anyhow, how do you ask him? He'll say for sure that we're trying to get rid of him, and steal all the glory."

Doc threw up his hands, and they went on around the beach to the east, passing the big colony of black gonies and the area of great boulders at the edge of the beach that Doc said harbored crayfish, and came to the turtle again. They were bloodied to the elbows when they'd finished, and took a swim to get clean once more before they cut around the edge of the lagoon to cross the island to the cottage with their steaks. When they were nearly home Geordie discovered that he was still carrying the flying fish that the frigate bird had contributed. They were dried out and seemed very unappetizing; Geordie decided that he would get more some other time, when he was coming straight back from the lagoon, and buried these in the sand. When they reached the cottage they all wrote down the number of rabbits they had shot on the board that Cap had hung up that morning. The total added up to one hundred eighty-six.

The turtle steaks were delicious, and even Catton complimented Geordie on them. "Really quite good, I must say."

"Thank you," Geordie said, surprised, and recalling Doc's advice added: "I'd like to help you skin some of the birds you collected today, if you want me to."

Catton's face took on a look of suspicion. "Why?" he

asked, and added: "In any event, I doubt you'd do it well

enough."

Geordie, who had been standing by the table, dropped back a step, and Cap said mildly; "Come, John. The boy was only offering to help."

"I've never seen a boy yet who wanted to do any work out of the goodness of his heart, and I'd thank you not to catch me up on anything I might want to say."

Cap didn't reply, and Catton got up, took a lantern, and went out of the cottage. No one said anything for a short time, and Doc and Cap looked at each other with worried creases in their foreheads.

"There really is something wrong with him," Doc said finally. "He was always unpleasant, but now he seems to be feeling persecuted."

"I don't see how I can send him back," Cap said unhappily. "We've got nothing, really, to justify it except a nasty disposition. So far, anyhow. He'd raise hell, and then his University would get into it and draw yours in, and there'd be one of those academic scandals that would give the newspapers a field day. All our dirty linen would be washed in public."

Doc had prepared Geordie for Catton's rebuff, but no one had prepared him for the situation that seemed to be developing and the concern shown by both Doc and Cap startled him. Nor had he heard before, in such plain terms, an exposition of the effects and the power of academic politics. This startled him even more, and for a long moment he was brought back to his father and his father's doubts about the satisfactions of the life that had so engaged him.

Doc and Cap had moved closer together and were talking seriously in undertones, and he knew they preferred to be alone at the moment. Doc glanced up at him.

"I think I'll develop the pictures I took today," Geordie said.

Doc nodded and Geordie went off to his room to work on the pictures. He began to arrange his equipment, but his movements grew slower and finally ceased as he thought of his first full day on the island. Until a few moments ago he had been quite excited; now the excitement was gone and a feeling of depression had taken its place. He sighed, and deciding to do the pictures tomorrow he put the equipment away and went to bed.

SEVENTEEN

The sun was shining when Geordie awoke the next morning; he dressed, and when he went into the living room there were several miller birds, finches, and a single honey eater busily flitting about. It was such a cheerful scene, so lively and normal, that the air of gloom at bedtime the night before seemed far away. Doc was sitting at the table with a piece of paper before him, drawing what appeared to be a plan; a miller bird landed on his shoulder and began to sing, and he looked up and grinned.

"Merry Christmas!" he said.

Geordie stared at him. "What?" he asked.

"Merry Christmas!" Doc repeated. "Did you forget what day it is?"

"I guess I did for the moment," Geordie said. "It still doesn't seem like that time of year."

"Cap brought a bottle of wine along for Christmas dinner. We'll have to do something special."

"I ought to make a cake," Geordie said. "I would if I had enough eggs."

"We'll have plenty of eggs later, when the terns nest. They nest on the south beach and an unusually high tide always washes their eggs away. When they lay again all the eggs are fresh, but I wouldn't know how to find fresh eggs anywhere now. I guess we'll have to settle for more turtle steaks."

"They were good. I'll go around the island this morning and see if I can find a turtle."

"Do that," Doc said. "The rest of us are going to plant the rest of the trees. We'll excuse you."

Geordie went around to the kitchen, and in company with two rails that ran about his feet cooked breakfast; after it was eaten he started for the freshwater pond. The air was full of birds coming in from the sea, for they fed early upon the squid that left the surface a little after dawn. He shot ten rabbits on the way and found eight ducks on the pond. Three of them were mallards, and flew off; he was surprised to see them there, and they reminded him of home. The other five were Laysan teal. He was very pleased to know that there were at least three more of them, and they seemed so tame that he decided to see if he could get them closer, remembering from his reading that they were inquisitive birds and recalled a trick Possum had once showed him, to entice them closer. He lay down on his belly in the bunch grass with his camera in front of him, and waved his feet in the air.

The teal swam back and forth and craned their necks; soon they began to move in. They came closer and closer, while Geordie held his breath. When he finally took several pictures of them they were only a few feet away. He stood up and moved off, quite pleased with himself, for he doubted that anyone had ever been so close to them before. He could develop the pictures after dinner and they would be a fine Christmas present to Doc.

As he walked toward the south beach he fell to thinking of home again and the activities of the season, the presents and the Christmas tree and people coming in rosy from the cold and the house fragrant with Ingrid's cooking, and of his mother and father. For a long moment he felt very lonely for all the things that were so far away, and then he came into the great cloud of terns and was so engaged by their airy multitude that he cheered up again. He decided to make a day of it alone even if he did find a turtle quickly, and went on.

As luck would have it he found a medium-sized turtle before he had gone very far. He turned it over and butchered it because the tide was coming in, cut out his steaks, and carrying them up the crest of the beach buried them deep in the sand to be picked up again later. He had a pleasant swim to clean himself up and went along the beach until he came to a big nesting colony of black gonies. This was their favorite nesting beach, which they liked more than the lagoon. There were thousands of them gathered there, many sitting on eggs, others without eggs sitting or wandering about. They were noisy, as usual, and some of them were dozing with their heads on their backs. Geordie sat down several feet from one of them, which looked at him calmly with its dark eyes, and he thought of them all, after the young had grown large enough to learn to take care of themselves, wandering on their narrow seven-foot wings over the trackless ocean as far as the Aleutians and back to find their island again.

The life of the colony went on around him. Birds took off for the sea, running and flapping for long distances before they were airborne, and others came in; there wasn't much wind, and most of these made clumsy landings, sometimes pitching forward and falling all over themselves. When they did this they would get up, collect themselves, look rather embarrassed, and waddle off; beautiful in the air, they were quite awkward on land. Presently another bird came in and waddled over to the one Geordie was near. It was the other one of the pair, come to relieve its mate after several days at sea. They made a ceremony of the changeover, touching beaks and talking to each other. The one on the egg was reluctant to leave, putting its head down mournfully; it was finally gently pushed off by the other, waddled away, and took to the air. Now that it had finally given up the egg, it might not return for eighteen or twenty days, during which time the bird on the egg would neither eat nor drink.

Geordie had lost track of the time, but the sun was getting higher and he decided to move on and spend some time with the Laysan albatrosses and other birds before going back to the cottage. He stood up, and turning away from the beach climbed the slight rise toward the middle of the island. The stunted bushes began and there seemed to be rabbits under all of them; he started to shoot them again. The little flightless rails ran about, he had to be careful not to break through into the numerous petrel burrows, and high over his head the rakish frigate birds were soaring on the warming air; they usually robbed the boobies in the early mornings and late afternoons. He decided to visit their roosting section later, on the way back, to collect some flying fish as an extra course at dinner, and went on to the portulaca flats around the lagoon.

The Laysan albatrosses, which outnumbered the black-footed ones, were nested in droves on the western side of the lagoon. There was a flock of a hundred or so golden plover, which nested on the Alaskan tundra and spent the winter on Laysan, on the open beach near the water; they didn't trust him and flew at his approach, whistling their lonely cries. There were a few bristle-thighed curlews too, also northern nesters, birds with long, down-curved bills, that were tamer. He came among the albatrosses and sat down again.

Unlike the black gonies, which only made slight depressions in the sand, the white birds built up their nests a little. Occasionally one of them would reach out, pick up a beakful of sand, and then pat it into the low walls with the side of the beak. The one nearest Geordie had a few weatherbeaten old bones around it, all that remained of a bird or two that had been killed long ago by the feather hunters. Many of them napped, and the unmated wandered idly about; presently, thirty or forty yards away, two of them began to dance.

They drew close together with great solemnity, bowing and almost stamping their feet, and circled facing each other, continuing to bow. They fenced a little with their beaks, whetting them upon each other; one of them raised a wing and nibbled at the feathers beneath it. The other bird stood like a statue while this was going on, and snapped its long hooked beak five or six times. The first bird stopped its nibbling, pointed its beak at the sky, rose up on its toes, puffed itself up, and gave a long, ridiculous, nasal groan; the other snapped its beak loudly and repeatedly. They both paused for a moment and began to bow rapidly to each other again.

It seemed as though they were going to go through the performance again and Geordie remembered his camera. He got up and approached them for a picture, but they didn't want their picture taken; they broke off their dance and separated and wandered away. Geordie was disappointed and waited for a time for another pair to begin, but none of them did; he finally decided that he would have to wait for another day. He threaded his way between them, pausing to pat one particularly benign-looking one, and continued around the north end of the lagoon to the frigate bird roost.

A number of these black pirates were sitting about on the stunted bushes and they looked at him calmly; Geordie was surprised to see several boobies nested on the ground immediately beneath them, and then decided that was the safest place for the boobies' young. The frigates couldn't get down through the bushes at them to pick the young boobies up when they hatched. Several of the frigates had big crops, and following Doc's procedure of the day before he found a stick and tapped them. As before, they regurgitated their fish, and Geordie collected a dozen good-sized ones, strung them on a stick, and walked back to the east beach and started along it for the cottage.

A fairy tern appeared above him and hovered, its wings translucent against the brilliant sky, the very picture of airiness and grace; then it dropped down in front of his face and hung staring at him with its big dark eyes, so close that he dropped his fish and raised his hand and caught it. It didn't struggle but lay quietly in his hand for a moment, a lovely bit of life, and as it rested there its mate came and hovered above Geordie's head and he let his captive go. He thought that they might be nested somewhere nearby, and decided that he would come back some day soon to see if he could find the nest.

He went along a little below the top of the ridge on the lagoon side, shooting rabbits as he went, recovered the turtle steaks, and cut around the end of the lagoon to the cottage. The surf on the reef and the changing colors of the ocean as the water deepened were beautiful. As he stood for a long moment looking out toward the empty horizon he thought that this was the strangest Christmas he had ever spent.

Catton was busy skinning birds in the warehouse workshop as he passed it, having apparently been out collecting, and Doc came out of the cottage.

"We'll have a cake after all," he said. "I was out doing in a few bunnies and came across a goney that had just laid an egg, so I pushed her off and took it. It's in the kitchen."

"I hope it's good."

"It will be very good. I ate a few of them before. They're so big that you get tired of eating them, but it will be just right for a cake."

"I saw five teal," Geordie said, but didn't mention the picture.

"Two went over me a little while after you'd left, so there must be seven. That's a good deal better than it seemed at first."

"It sure is. I'd better get to the kitchen and start my cake."

"When you get things under control, come find me. We'll take a Christmas swim."

Christmas dinner went off very well with the exception of Cap's wine, which had gone sour.

"Too bad, too, after the chef has made such heroic efforts," Cap said ruefully. "I guess I should have averaged it, and brought two bottles. One of them might have been good. Well, we can't have everything, and we do have rabbits."

"We have two hundred and ninety-six less than we had when we got here," Doc said. "I was checking the board just before I sat down. That's good, but it's not good enough. We'll have to bear down harder. Maybe we should eat a few of them."

Everyone looked so unenthusiastic at this that he discarded the idea. "I doubt I could eat one myself," he said. "But we will have to work harder at killing them."

"Yes," Cap said. "Everybody remember."

Catton spoke up. "While we're on the subject of shooting," he said, "I'd like permission to shoot a pair of Laysan teal. I seem to recall, Cap, that you forbade it. But we don't have a specimen, and the University—"

"I'm sorry, John, but I can't allow it. Only two have been seen so far, and it might mean their extinction."

Neither Geordie nor Doc said anything about the others they had seen, for they thought it would only stir Catton up needlessly; Catton scowled.

"They will probably die anyhow, and be lost," he said. "I think your attitude is rather silly."

He stared angrily at Cap, and Geordie, wanting to be out of the room if an unpleasant argument should develop, hastily excused himself and went to develop his pictures. As he worked he could hear the rumble of voices around the table, and then he heard Catton stamp angrily to his room. A silence followed; Geordie finally had his negatives done, and was very pleased with them. He waved them around to dry, and went back into the living room again.

"I have a Christmas present for you," he said, and gave the negatives of the teal to Doc. Doc held them up and squinted through them toward the light.

"These are really splendid," he said finally, and thrust out the finger; he hadn't done that for a long time. "If the teal vanish, as they well might, these will be the best pictures ever taken of them. Don't tell me if you don't want to, but how did you get so close?"

"I think I'll keep it a secret," Geordie said smiling.

"It's a trick Possum showed me."

"Possum? Oh, that fellow in the marsh. He's certainly done well by you," Doc said, and then recalled that Geordie knew nothing of Uncle Harry's maneuverings. "You can tell him when you get home," he added hastily.

"The moon's almost full. Want to take a walk?"

"Yes, sir."

"Get your rifle and flashlight, and meet me out front."

The petrels were in the air in great numbers, their pale breasts glimmering as they flitted through the moonlight, their odd, low, growling notes rising and falling; sometimes one would hover close, and this would always be startling. They would appear in front of the face as though by magic, hang for a moment on flickering wings, and magically vanish, leaving the echo of their kitten-like growling in the ears.

"There must be thousands of them here," Doc said. "They're eerie little devils. It's like moving around through the spirits of the departed. I'm glad my conscience is clear."

With the pale birds flitting about them they cut across toward the southeastern beach. They came to a sandy area where the ground was honeycombed with petrel burrows, and to find their way through it without going in to their knees they used their flashlights occasionally. The flashlight beams picked up a number of burrows that had pairs of birds sitting together in their openings, and as Doc and Geordie drew close they would scramble out, sometimes blundering into the men's legs, growling, and vanish. The white tails of retreating rabbits moved off through the moonlight, and sometimes they could get close enough to shoot one; there was an occasional scurry of rails.

They came out on the beach north of the roosting

terns; the surf tossed its gleaming white crests high against the broken glitter of the dark ocean, and walking along the beach they were soon at the edge of the nesting black gonies. The dark birds dotted the pale sand; Doc and Geordie climbed a little above them, and as they stood looking out over them a pair approached each other not far from the water's edge, bowing, the preliminary of a dance. They were joined by several others. The thunder of the surf drowned out their groanings, but their posturing, in perfect unison, lighted by the moon and carried on against the backdrop of the breaking waves, was like an uncanny ballet.

When they finally broke off, another pair, a little further away, began to dance. Doc and Geordie were so intent upon watching the strange scene, at once eerie and enthralling, that they didn't notice the clouds racing in behind them and the rising wind. Soon the moon was swallowed up, the wind increased to gale force, and it began to rain, and almost immediately the rain turned into a roaring downpour that blotted out everything beyond a few yards away.

They shouted to each other, and stumbling out onto the beach again hurried south. The rain walled them in; their flashlights showed them little except the silvery surrounding raindrops and they stayed close to the edge of the water. On the south beach they lost it for a little and stumbled into some of the roosting terns, which rose wildly around them until they found the water's edge again. They went on, until they began to wonder if they hadn't passed the cottage, for the wind, coming from the west, blinded them with flying spray as well as rain. A lull came in the storm, and they saw the lights and stumbled up the little grade and went into the workshop and took off their dripping clothes.

They ran into the house for towels; Cap and Catton

had gone to bed and the only occupant of the living room was a finch asleep on the back of a chair. Its head appeared from under a wing; it regarded them drowsily, chirped once, tucked its head back again.

"Holy Poseidon!" Doc said, as he dried himself. "It was almost as bad as the blizzard that nearly killed us. We'd better take the rifles apart and dry and oil them. I've never been so wet, but it was worth it while it lasted."

"It sure was," Geordie said. "I was thinking this morning what a strange Christmas it was, but I hadn't seen anything yet. The petrels, and the albatrosses dancing in the moonlight . . . I'll never forget it the rest of my life."

"Amen," Doc said.

The rain began again with a roar, and they began to dismantle the rifles.

EIGHTEEN

It rained all night and all the next day; the heavy recurring showers marched across the sea and the sodden island, with intervals of lighter rain between them. The wind was cold and gusty, occasionally so high that spray from the ocean was flung against the house like hail, for the waves came far up the beach. By afternoon everyone except Catton, who had taken himself to the warehouse to work on skins and requested that they let him alone, was finished with his chores and at loose ends. Doc had completed the plan he was drawing, which he revealed to be for a pen for rails; he had decided to catch about a hundred of them and take them to Midway when they stopped there on the way home.

"It will be better to have them two places than one," he said. "If it happens that they don't survive here, maybe they'll manage to do it at Midway."

"Can't we catch some of the honey eaters and miller birds too?" Geordie asked.

"I don't think we could catch enough of them to make it worthwhile," Doc said. "If they just ran around like the rails we could chase them and catch them in nets, but, alas, they can fly. I doubt it would be any use transplanting a few of them. You need a good nucleus, what with the right sex ratios, the accidents of life, and so on." He began to wander around restlessly. "I think I'll put on raingear and take a walk. Anybody want to go?"

"I think I'll take a nap," Cap said. "It's too cold to get wet, and I never got enough sleep on destroyers."

"I'll go," Geordie said, and went to get his sou'wester.

They set out, heading for the lagoon. They had their rifles with them and shot some rabbits but not as many as they would have liked, for many of them had crawled into petrel burrows to get out of the rain. As they came over the height of land on the western side of the lagoon they began to find many of the petrel burrows blown shut, and several times they found petrels that had managed to get their heads out but nothing else; the sand held them captive, and most of them were exhausted and beaten by the weather.

"You see what's happened," Doc said. "There's been so much of the vegetation eaten up that there's not enough left to stabilize the sand any more. There's going to be a big loss of birds every time there's a bad wind."

They dug out the birds whose heads were showing when they came across them, and in walking about to do this broke through into burrows frequently; some of the birds they dug out were too far gone to survive. They were wet and cold and covered with damp, sticky sand that itched by the time they could look over the lagoon. The rain had raised the water level considerably; many of the white goney nests had been built high enough to be just above it, but many more were awash and had been deserted. Eggs were floating about, many gonies were standing around disconsolately, having lost their nests, and there were a number of bristle-thighed curlews making the most of the calamity; they were busily eating eggs or carrying them off in their long bills.

"Glum sight," Doc said. "But we'll come back when the rain stops and collect some of the eggs, and blow them. I can always use them to trade with other museums which don't have them. I think I'm cold enough now to go back. How about you?"

"I am too," Geordie said. He was shivering, and ready to call it a day. "Do you think," he said, as they were walking back, "that it would be all right if I collected a few birds and prepared them for our museum? I know you brought a good collection of skins and eggs back when you were here before, but there must have been some things you didn't get."

"I think it would be a fine idea," Doc said. "We'll clear it with Cap, just as a matter of form, but I'm all for it. There are a number of species that move in and out of here that I didn't get, and they should be represented; maybe the taxonimists can make new subspecies out of them. We don't have too many skins of some of the birds here anyhow; we should send the National Museum a few more, and have a few extras ourselves. I'll make up a list of the ones we have enough of, and you can work on the rest. I'd rather you got them than I; I don't feel much like collecting on this trip, somehow. I'd rather just look and take notes and photographs. I'll have enough to do. We're going to take a goney census, I want to make a series of slides of blood films to see what the parasites are here, and so on. And shoot the cussed rabbits." He saw a rabbit, stopped, and shot it. "I don't know why I call them cussed rabbits. It's not their fault that they're wrecking the place. I always sort of admired rabbits, in a way. They're pretty defenseless, all predators live on them, but they've been around a long time and with everything against them have managed to survive. They're a successful species, but they've got no business being here. What's the total so far?"

"I looked as I came out," Geordie said. "What with the ones we've shot this afternoon it's about three hundred and fifty."

"Hardly scratches the surface. You saw what's been done to the petrels; presently it will be the honey eaters, the miller birds, and the rails, whose food supply will be gone. I think we'd better plan to make a special hunt every day, spreading out and marching the length of the island in addition to the offhand execution that we do."

"Yes, sir," Geordie said, remembering the sand-plugged petrel burrows and the birds they had dug out. "I think we'd better."

The next morning the sun was out again and they went back to the lagoon and waded around and collected eggs. The curlews had gotten there before them but they managed to get three dozen eggs. They drilled holes in both ends of each egg and blew the contents out. The little rails discovered what was going on and gathered around to eat the contents, running over their legs eagerly and squabbling with each other as they sat working on the sand.

A few evenings later, a little after sunset, KITTIWAKE appeared and stood off the island. It was too late for a landing, and as the sea was calm she anchored to await the morning. They packed the eggs, exposed film, and bird skins that Catton had prepared to go back on her. Before he went to bed Geordie walked around the cottage and looked at her lights riding well beyond the reef and thought of other times when the Japanese had appeared, probably to anchor in the same place, and come ashore to stay for awhile to slaughter thousands of birds for feathers for women's hats. It had been a wasteful and heartless business, and he could imagine the little men running about with their clubs along the eastern beach and the shores of the lagoon, smashing down the albatrosses on their nests and cutting off their wings, letting them lie beside their eggs to bleed to death.

He saw too the birds they had crippled and thrown into the cistern to crawl over each other and bleed and starve. He felt a little sick as he thought of it, and wondered how anyone, after watching the beautiful, gliding flight of an albatross or looking into its calm, dark eyes, could do such things. There were some creatures in the world, like the unfortunate rabbits, that had to be controlled; but the sea birds (including the lovely little fairy terns and any others that the raiders had been able to catch) harmed nothing. They were expressions of life in its infinite variety and beauty, and defenseless in their inexperience of the wasteful cruelty of men. Geordie discovered that his fists were clenched as he thought of those Japanese; he hated them, and was very glad that the men from KITTIWAKE had caught them and taken them in. They were not, however, the only offenders; many Americans had done things as reprehensible, slaughtering game for the market or just because it was there, emptying the plains of buffalo for their hides or their tongues.

Before Geordie turned away to go back into the cottage he determined that he would try, in some way before he was dead, to show them what dreadful things they were doing and get them to stop it. He didn't know, now, what he would do or how he would do it; but he was sure that it would come to him as he learned more.

The ship's boat brought the captain ashore the next morning; he spent an hour or so and left again, taking the material they had packed with him. Geordie had heard no more about the possibility of sending Catton back and when Catton went north on the island and the boat left without him it was evident that Cap had given up the idea. There wasn't, as Cap had said before, any real reason to do it except the nasty disposition, and in any event Catton hadn't made any scenes lately or caused any trouble. He did, certainly, seem to withdraw even more, but that was no reason to get rid of him.

The three of them watched KITTIWAKE weigh anchor and steam away and turned to the day's occupations. They had built up the fire again after breakfast to give KITTIWAKE's captain coffee, and as there was still a little life in the embers Geordie decided to make some cookies; so he built up the fire again. He worked with the rails and miller birds hunting around him and a honey eater singing from the roof, and when the cookies were finished he picked up his rifle and camera and went rabbit hunting.

He went eastward across the island and shot a large number of rabbits on the way, for they were out in force now that the sun had appeared again. The air was lively with birds and he turned northward when he reached the height of land above the lagoon; he stopped to watch a pair of frigate birds above the ocean. They were soaring very high in the air, black and rakish; when they soared their long forked tails were sometimes folded together to make points, and this, with their long, narrow, pointed wings, like somewhat flattened M's, added to their rakish appearance. They were superb fliers, admirably equipped for flight; Doc had told Geordie that their pectoral muscles made up about a quarter of their body weight and that their tails alone were controlled by seven pairs of strong muscles. Not even hurricanes, which drove such fine fliers as albatrosses down onto the beach, seemed to disturb them. Although it was a bit late in the morning for boobies to be coming back with fish they were waiting for one, and presently they saw it. They rolled over, backed their wings, and came down out of the sky like meteors; it was a thrilling thing to watch. Geordie unconsciously rose on his toes in the excitement of it. The booby couldn't have gotten away from one of them, much less two; they seemed to be everywhere about it at once, and made short work of its attempts to escape them. It disgorged its fish which the pair of them, seeming to merge in their swift maneuvers, picked out of the air.

Still tingling from the sight, Geordie went out onto the beach and turned north, between the nesting black gonies and the surf. He didn't stop to watch them this morning, for he had remembered the fairy tern and wanted to see if he could find its nest. When he came to the place where he had caught one of them several days before the bird appeared again over his head, so pale and translucent against the sky that it seemed almost like a ghost, a disembodied spirit with large dark eyes. As before it dropped down in front of him to stare at his face, grunting low, and he could have caught it again.

He turned up into the dying scaevola bushes and began to look about; suddenly he found the young one sitting on top of a piece of phosphate rock. It was a tiny, downy little thing, grayish brown, with a black patch on its head and two dark stripes on its back, with a short bluish bill and rather large, strongly clawed feet. It needed these claws, for fairy terns build no nest; they lay their eggs on a rock or the horizontal limb of a tree, and the young one has to cling to its precarious place from the time it is hatched.

Geordie, much engaged with it, sat down two or three feet away and unslung his camera. The nestling looked at him with interest but without fear, and he took several pictures of it. Just as he started to put his camera away one of the parents came in, accepted him without hesitation, and landed beside the chick. There were seven very small fish in its beak, held crosswise one after another, and Geordie hardly had time to wonder how the bird had managed to catch and carry them that way before the chick moved close and took the first one. The others were moved forward as the chick took the one at the tip of the beak; it was an extraordinary performance, and Geordie was so fascinated by it and by the sleek and gentle beauty of the old bird that he forgot to take more pictures. For a moment he was irritated at himself, and then realized that he would have many more opportunities. He waited until the old bird had flown off and got up and went south between the lagoon and the western beach.

His day's total of rabbits was fifty-one by the time he met Cap, who was also out shooting them, about halfway down the island. Cap had shot twenty-nine; they joined forces and zigzagged back and forth until they reached the cottage where they posted a grand total of ninety-six.

"Our best day, by far," Cap said. "We'll have to try to keep it at that level. You certainly did well today."

"Yes, sir. You know, it's a funny thing. I thought I was shooting a lot of them, and then after Doc and I dug out the petrels, when I saw what was happening to them because the rabbits have eaten so much of the vegetation, I seemed to shoot more."

"I know what you mean," Cap said. "I saw some of the petrels after the storm, and I seemed to shoot more rabbits too. Maybe we weren't doing as well as we could until we had an actual demonstration of the damage. We were dragging our feet a little, whether we realized it or not."

"I won't drag them any more," Geordie said.

"No. Neither will I. We'll take another march late in the afternoon."

They found Doc in the workshop, and all had some lunch. Geordie told Doc about the fairy tern's nest.

"I'll go back there with you in the morning," Doc said. "That bird's a little early, and probably the only one on the island with a chick. We'll both get pictures. I'd tell John about it, but he might want to take the chick. We'll just save this one for ourselves, and let it grow up." He grinned. "The tide will be all the way out in an hour or so. Why don't we go fishing on the reef?"

This sounded like a fine idea, and they all agreed. An hour later, wearing nothing but their shoes, they got into the small boat that KITTIWAKE had left them that morning and went out to the reef. The footing was not very dependable and when the higher waves came in they were up to their waists and had to watch their balance, but the fishing was good. Geordie was enjoying himself immensely when suddenly, after the crest of a wave had passed, he was gripped around one leg. Startled, he looked down. An octopus, a foot or two long, had come in on the wave and wrapped several of its tentacles around him. Swaying, gray, and rubbery, staring with its flat black eye, it filled him with a shocked, cold horror that momentarily paralyzed him; then, with a yell, he kicked it with his other foot. It discharged a cloud of ink, turned loose of him, and scudded off.

Doc and Cap both floundered toward him. By the time they got there he had recovered from his fright and was laughing a little shakily, somewhat embarrassed by the uproar he had made; the creature's sucking discs had left red welts on his leg.

"Are you all right?" Doc asked, coming up. "What was it?"

"An octopus," Geordie said. "It startled . . . it really scared the devil out of me. It wasn't big enough to do much harm, but it took hold and I looked down, and . . . Ugh! I guess I'll do my fishing from the boat, for the rest of this trip."

He shivered a little from the memory of that cold, impersonal eye, so alien and so different from the expressive eyes of birds and animals, but by the time Doc and Cap joined him in the boat again he was smiling about his adventure. They all laughed about it on the way to shore, cleaned their fish at the water's edge, and went up to the cottage. They had had a good afternoon and were feeling pleasantly tired and at peace with the world until they came around the corner of the house and found Catton on the porch. He put his hands on his hips and glowered at them; they all stopped and looked at him.

"Celebrating, eh?" he asked. His eyes narrowed.

"Celebrating what, John?" Cap asked. "Did you have a good day?"

"Oh, I had a fine day. Why wouldn't I? I had plenty of time to think about the fine trick you played on me."

"Trick?" Cap asked, in a puzzled voice. "What trick? What's on your mind, John?"

"Do you think I don't know you sent the Laysan teal skins back on the ship? Do you take me for a complete ass? After forbidding . . . forbidding, I repeat, me from shooting those birds you got them yourselves, for your museum, and now you can laugh at me. Laugh, then. You won't do much laughing later."

There was a startled silence, and Cap and Doc stared flabbergasted at each other. Finally Doc said: "Nobody has shot teal or sent skins anywhere, John. Good heavens, man, where did you get that idea?"

"The teal weren't there when I came down today. I saw this . . . this kid," he said, pointing to Geordie, "a day or two ago, lying by the fresh water pool, waving his legs in the air to entice the teal into range. Oh," he went on, his voice rising, "I see it all. Ringing in this innocent looking little devil, thinking I wouldn't pay any attention to him."

"I was taking pictures," Geordie said.

Catton looked at him with such venom that he fell back a step. "Taking pictures!" Catton said. "Very likely!" His voice rose again, his face flushed, and he clenched his fists. "Taking pictures! Taking me for a—"

"Enough of that!" Cap rapped out, in a tone that must have made sailors quake in the past. "Stow that sort of talk, and come with me. We'll go to the pond right now."

He started off, and after glaring at his back for a moment Catton went after him. Geordie and Doc stood and watched them go.

"I'll be drawn and quartered," Doc said. "And the ship no sooner out of sight. So that's how you got so close to those teal."

"I didn't know he was anywhere around. I didn't see him. Doc, what's the matter with him?"

Doc shook his head. "I think we'd better keep sort of an eye on him from now on, but we can talk more about this with Cap."

"Yes, sir," Geordie said unhappily, for Catton's venomous look and the fact that Catton had been trailing him about and watching him, as well as the man's accusation that he had been brought along as an accomplice to underhand maneuvers, upset him a good deal. The accusation was so false as to be unbalanced, and Geordie had never had any dealings with unbalanced people; he didn't know how to estimate them or what they might do.

He and Doc sat on the front steps until Cap and Catton came back. Catton went into the house without looking at anyone; Cap sat down with them.

"There were five teal there," Cap said, "so I think we've got that business quieted down." He looked at Geordie for a moment, thoughtfully. "We'll have to . . ." he began, and broke off and turned to Doc. "I'd like to talk to you a little about all this later."

NINETEEN

In the morning, Doc and Geordie went off to the fairy tern's nest, to get more pictures. Geordie was rather silent; he had thought a good deal about Catton in the night, and had gotten nowhere. As they walked along the western beach Doc, who had been rather quiet too, finally broke the silence.

"Cap and I took a walk after you'd gone to your room," he said. "We're both disturbed about that affair yesterday, for John got you involved in it."

"He doesn't like me,' Geordie said. "He hasn't liked me from the first."

"I don't think you liked him either. You might think that you didn't like him because of the way he reacted to you, but you might have felt the same way if he'd been pleasant. For two people to dislike each other at sight isn't an extraordinary occurrence; it happens all the time, and no one else can explain it."

Geordie hadn't thought of this; it had never occurred to him, and he didn't know what to reply.

"He probably felt that," Doc went on, "but all this is beside the point, more or less. The point is that something has happened or is happening inside John's head, and changing him. I think he's on his way to a mental condition. I'm not a doctor; I don't know what it is or where it's liable to go; he ought to be under treatment, but that's not possible. We've got him on our hands, and we'll have to do the best we can. We'll have to watch him carefully and compare notes about what we see. He might get more . . . troublesome, and he might not. If he does we'll have to take care of it when we come to it. But he doesn't like Cap, who he thinks is not letting him do some things he wants to do, and he doesn't like you, and you'll have to be careful not to give him an opportunity to dislike you more. Keep an eye out and don't spend any more time than you have to by yourself. Have somebody else in sight if you can."

"I will," Geordie said. He had been thinking of the situation as very unpleasant but now, even though Doc had deliberately underplayed it, he realized that it might become dangerous. He was shocked and then angry that such a cloud had appeared over the island's fine, carefree life and would now continue to be there.

"It won't help any to be sore about it," Doc said, catching his expression. "That will just make it worse. Make up your mind to accept it and live with it."

"Yes," Geordie said, abashed, and by the time they

had walked the rest of the way to the tern's nesting place he was trying to make the adjustment.

He didn't make it that day; it didn't come easy for him, or all at once. For the next few evenings, as he lay in his cot before falling asleep, he struggled with it and learned some things about himself. It was difficult at first to accept Doc's remark that he might have been at fault too, with an unconscious but evident dislike of Catton; it had never occurred to him before to blame himself for the way people felt toward him. They had either liked or disliked him, and he had let it go at that. He began to see that this view was too simple and self-centered, and it was time he grew out of it. He had also fumed inwardly at being restricted even though the restriction was a comparatively mild one, and he realized that this was self-centered too. They would all be restricted; he wasn't the only one; and instead of withdrawing and letting Doc and Cap look out for him he should be looking out for them as well as himself.

As these things grew clearer to him he came to accept Catton as the others accepted him, and to lose his hostility; Catton was a sick man and it was silly to be mad at him. A few days later Cap gave him permission to collect a few of the birds that weren't permanent residents of the island, and the first one he shot was a gull the like of which he hadn't seen before. He didn't know what it was, and when he took it into the workshop, where Doc and Catton were working, Catton asked to see it. Geordie gave it to him.

"I think it's a Bonaparte's gull," he said, after he had examined it. "There's no previous record of one here." He held it, looking at it longingly.

Geordie realized that he wanted it badly; he glanced at Doc, who nodded slightly. "I'll give it to you, if you want it," he said.

Catton looked at him and blinked and looked again; Geordie could almost see him thinking, wondering what sort of trick was being played on him. There hadn't been an incident since the affair of the teal to arouse his suspicions, but he clung to them. "Why?" he asked finally.

"I think you want it very much," Geordie said, "and your collection's more important than mine."

"I'm glad somebody realizes that," Catton said. "I'll take it, only don't expect anything in return."

"I won't.

"And don't think that this will make me relax my vigilance," he said, and turned away to the skinning table.

Doc and Geordie went out, to go rabbit hunting.

"Well," Doc said, "you made a try. Don't remind him of it any time, though, or he'll be sure it was for some ulterior purpose." He shook his head, and added: "I was very pleased to see you offer it to him."

For a time Catton seemed a little better; he worked hard and kept to himself and found nothing to quarrel about. They all hoped that this would continue, but they watched him and tried to keep someone in view when they were moving around. They worked harder at shooting rabbits and by early January had killed close to twelve hundred of them, but despite this there seemed to be as many as before and the more intelligent ones among them were growing warier.

Their lives fell into a loose routine of rabbit hunting, photography, observation, a little collecting on Geordie's part, and swimming or fishing parties limited to the three of them in the afternoons when the weather was clear and warm enough. They did more fishing on the reef, and several times went out to collect good pieces of coral. Geordie began to hunt for shells on the beach, and gathered a collection, including some very fine cowries. The sooty terns appeared in greater numbers, and the noddies began to lay. More gonies came in off the sea, and after the storm, which had flooded out a number of nests, some of the albatrosses that hadn't suffered built their nests higher. Doc saw the first phalarope. The petrels were laying eggs or brooding eggs already laid and didn't fill the air any more at night.

Around the twenty-first of the month Doc reported that the first goney had hatched, and by the twenty-third there were a lot of young gonies. Geordie, who, when he wasn't shooting rabbits, had been spending a lot of time among the gonies, taking pictures of them and letting them nibble the buttons on his shirt cuffs, the bright screws on his tripod, and even his fingers, had to move off a little, especially from the black gonies. Now that the fuzzy, dark gray young were out of the eggs their parents, who had calmly allowed all sorts of liberties, became very belligerent. They would lunge out, snapping the hooked beaks that were capable of opening an artery, sometimes growing so excited that they would regurgitate their last meal; occasionally one would charge with extended wings, snapping as they came for him. They brooded the young for a few days, and for several weeks after that took turns shielding them from the hot midday sun. As the young grew older they began to move clumsily around a little, waiting for their parents to return, and Geordie often wondered how the old birds managed to pick them out of so many others. They were always hungry and would pester any adult bird for food, begging and wheezing; strange adults would often peck them viciously, but it didn't seem to discourage them. They were fed by regurgitation; their parents would stand over them, open their bills, and let the half-digested food drip into their waiting beaks.

Doc wanted to take an albatross census, and they divided the island into quarters and spent several days

counting. When they were finished they built the pen for the rails. It would have been easy to start their captures with the ones that ran about the house, but none of them wanted to do that; they all liked the little birds around, and went further afield for them. The greatest number of them seemed to be around the lagoon, where they chased them with nets; it was a tiring and dusty business, for in the heat of the chase they would often break through into petrel burrows and flounder about up to their waists.

When Geordie had time between these enterprises and his cooking and rabbit hunting and general wandering about to watch the changing scene he did some collecting on his own and prepared the skins, for he wanted to give them to the University when he got home. There was a fairly constant population of migrant birds which spent the winter on Laysan: bristle-thighed curlews, Pacific golden plover, and European turnstones; others, such as phalaropes, sanderlings, black-bellied plover, and Siberian whimbrels wandered through the island chain, occasionally appearing and rare in any case. There was a romantic aura about them, for several made tremendous migrations from Siberia or Alaska to New Zealand and back again; besides that, they were wary and difficult to approach, unlike the sea birds and the birds of Laysan. Skill was required to get within range of them and to hit them, and it was exciting not only to find and identify them but to collect and prepare their skins.

Geordie patrolled the beaches and the lagoon with the shotgun when he had a chance in the hope of finding a rare specimen, but he didn't have the gun the day he saw a black-bellied plover on the shore of the lagoon; he had been rabbit hunting with his rifle, and they didn't often shoot rabbits with the shotgun. Doc had told him that this bird had never been recorded on Laysan, and it would be quite a feather in his cap if he could get it; he ran all the way back to the cottage for the gun, burst in through the door, and was startled to find Catton sitting sprawled on a chair with his head on the table. Catton sat up groggily; he was a bad color, and shaking, and had vomited several times.

"I'm sick," he mumbled. "I'm sick."

He let his head fall with a thump to the tabletop again. Geordie had a moment of panic, and then collected himself. He ran up to Catton and leaned over him. "Can I help you to bed?" he asked anxiously. "Do you want anything?"

"No, no," Catton said blearily. "Get Doc, get somebody."

Geordie stood in indecision for a moment, afraid to leave the man and afraid not to leave him for help; finally he decided to find either Doc or Cap and ran out of the house. There was no one in sight in any direction, and Geordie's heart sank; both Doc and Cap might be at the other end of the island. He decided that the best thing he could do would be to go toward the lagoon and get on the height of land around it, and trotted off in that direction. As luck would have it he was only halfway there when he saw them both come over the skyline; they had been at the lagoon and were coming home, and he shouted at them and put on speed. They began to hurry when they saw him running, and when he met them and told them about Catton they fell into a trot.

They were nearly at the cottage when Doc said: "There's no use of your coming in too, Geordie. Cap and I can take care of things."

"I saw a black-bellied plover," Geordie said. "I came back to get the gun and found him. If there's nothing I can do to help I think I'll go and get it."

"Yes," Doc said. "I'll hand you out the gun, and you take off." When he brought out the gun he looked concerned. "He hasn't any temperature," he said, "so it's not an infection of any sort. It can't be anything he ate, for we've all eaten the same food. The only thing I can think of is that he's got a dose of arsenic poisoning, and that's serious. He probably was already carrying some that he's been absorbing through his pores, and then eaten more by mistake or carelessness, and that's touched off a real attack. We'll try to wash him out and keep him quiet. Go ahead and get the plover if you can; you can give us a hand when you come back."

Geordie went off toward the lagoon, rather frightened by Doc's diagnosis, for he knew how dangerous arsenic poisoning could be. Catton knew too, but he had been working on a large number of skins and in his disturbed condition had probably been careless. He might die, and Geordie had never been so close to possible death before. He thought of everything around him—the sun, the wind, the island's overflowing life, the lovely shades of the ocean and the surf on the reef—being blotted out, and shuddered.

Several minutes later he was distracted from his thoughts by two red-tailed tropic birds that flew past him with their rapid, steady wingbeats, satiny white with a pale pinkish cast and striking red bills, playing together in the air. They were evidently courting, for in their swift, pigeon-like flight they milled about, dove, stalled, and even flew backwards, squawking, always maintaining an exact distance from each other. Once or twice the upper one, apparently the male, would bend his two long, red, spike-like tail feathers straight down to touch the bird below. They were so pretty and so extraordinary in their maneuvering that by the time they were gone Geordie had forgotten his thoughts of death.

He was delighted to have seen their airy dance, for he had heard about it and been afraid that he would not; there weren't many on Laysan, for they liked heavy cover to nest in, and the height of their nesting season was May or June. They were awkward on the ground and walked badly, but were wonderful in the air; not even the frigate, for all their superior flying, could bother them very much.

He went on, thinking about them and hoping that he would presently find a nest to photograph, and came to the lagoon. The young gonies were wandering or sitting on their tails with their feet in front of them and there was much activity among their parents; the plover was still in the same place but flew before Geordie got within range. He followed it almost to the northern end of the lagoon before he finally got a shot and killed it, and not wanting to go back right away kept on around the end of the lagoon until he came to the frigate's rookery.

A few of them were beginning to nest and the males, with long, green, iridescent scapular feathers, now had the big red sacs below their beaks inflated like footballs and were sitting on the bushes to guard the sticks that the females brought them, for they stole nesting material from each other when they could. The sacs were the male's chief attraction; when the female of his choice appeared over his head he would stand up and display them. They were, Geordie thought, a strange and somewhat ridiculous inducement and awkward to handle in the air, but the females seemed to be impressed by them. While Geordie watched, a female came down; the male rose up on the nest and leaned backwards and the female landed and imitated him. Facing each other, they raised their hooked beaks, spread their wings, and rolled their heads and their bodies. They gurgled and chuckled; the male's green scapulars rose like bristles, and both birds

puffed themselves up, trembled, and finally mated on the nest.

Geordie turned away presently and started back. He hoped that now the frigates had started nesting he would be able to get pictures of their antics. To make better time he went out onto the beach. The tide was very low, lower than he had ever seen it, and he went out and poked about the boulders that were usually awash; in the deep pools around them he could see many big crayfish moving around but had no way to catch them; he thought of rigging up a long-handled net to be ready if the tide fell so low again. Further south he saw a flock of red phalaropes come in off the sea and head for the lagoon. All of the migrating birds should be increasing now, and more of the terns, both graybacks and noddies, should be coming in to nest. He turned over a big turtle on the beach near the end of the lagoon, and not having his knife with him cut across the island to get it and return.

Doc was sitting on the steps, with his rifle beside him; he'd been out shooting rabbits. "We've got him in bed," he said, to Geordie's inquiring look. "When we got him undressed we found his arms and legs all broken out. It's arsenical poisoning as sure as the devil. Cap's with him now; we're going to take turns."

"I'll take a turn too," Geordie said. "At least, I can holler if I need help or don't know what to do."

"No need for you to do it," Doc said. "I think we can keep you busy enough. Cap and I talked it over awhile ago. If John is laid up for long, or if he . . . doesn't make it, his collection will have to be filled. Cap can't skin a bird, and that will leave it up to you and me to collect and work up all the skins for John's university, the ones we want, and the ones for the National Museum. We have rails to catch, pictures to take, some sets of eggs to collect, and rabbits to shoot. I looked on the board awhile ago, and to date we've shot close to three thousand of them and they're getting wilder all the time, so our average will probably go down from now on. We're a long, long way from cleaning them out, and we've only got about five more weeks to go. I'll be out of circulation part of the time and Cap can help with the rabbits when he's free, but you can see that you'll be doing a lot of work. I'm sorry, Geordie. It won't be quite as leisurely for any of us as we thought it would."

"It's been pretty easy so far," Geordie said. "It's been sort of like a vacation, with plenty of time to look around. I don't mind working a lot harder, Doc. I'd like to do it. I hope I can fix the skins well enough."

"You'll do," Doc said. "Let's go out and shoot some more rabbits."

"I have a turtle on the east beach. I've got to go butcher him."

"Get your rifle and put the plover away," Doc said. "I'll go along."

When they returned they found Cap sitting on the steps, and he got up and walked toward them. They all stopped a few yards from the cottage.

"He's very sick," Cap said. "We didn't always have a doctor handy on destroyers, so I had to know a little medicine, and we'll just have to do the best we can. I've been thinking about the situation and I've decided it would be best if you, Geordie, stayed away from him. It would be unpleasant for you to help us nurse him, and unnecessary, and it might stir him up. From one or two things he's mumbled I take it he still thinks about that business of the teal once in awhile. He's pretty confused and I want to avoid confusing him more. You don't mind?"

"No, sir, I sure don't. I'd be glad to help, but I guess you're right that it's better I stay out of his sight. Doc's given me some work to do, anyhow.

"Good," Cap said.

TWENTY

The first thing Geordie did the next morning was to go through Catton's skins and eggs to see what he had collected, and to check over his lists to see how many specimens of everything he had intended to get. He was glad to see that the native birds, the honey eaters, miller birds, rails, and finches were about well enough represented already and not many more were needed, for he had never wanted to kill any of them. Their tameness, the pleasure they had given him around the cottage, and the fact that they might be on the edge of extinction had set them apart for him. He knew that they should be represented in several museums, especially if they might vanish from the earth, but that didn't make any difference; he just didn't want to collect them.

He was full of admiration for the skins that were there, for they were beautifully done; he hoped that some day he would be as expert as Catton. The man was universally disliked, and with good reason, but he was a master of his work; even lately, despite his disturbed condition, his work was faultless. It was depressing that he had always been so difficult, and more depressing still that he might die on this lonely island and his talents be lost.

Geordie turned away from this thought and tried to lay out a tentative schedule for himself. The basis of his days, he thought, would be to make rabbit patrols in the mornings and evenings with the rifle, and another for specimens with the shotgun in the middle of the day, for it was then that most birds were less active and liable to be resting where he could get at them. He would work on skins in the evenings after dinner. He knew that this would vary, and many times he would wish he had the shotgun when he had the rifle and the other way around, but that couldn't be helped. He should always have a camera with him, and there would be time on all the patrols to search for nests, watch the life about him, and so on. For a moment, harking back to Doc's advice to have someone always in view he wondered how he was going to do it; then he realized that this wasn't necessary any more, and felt pleasantly free.

Having gone over all this in his mind he decided to start off, for there was an air of gloomy apprehension about the cottage and he wanted to get away from it. He went in to get the rifle and the camera and found Doc finishing his breakfast; Doc had watched beside Catton part of the night, and slept late. "He's not good," Doc said. "I think I'll go with you, if you're going out."

They left in a somewhat subdued frame of mind, and headed for the freshwater pond; when they were nearly there Doc suddenly stopped. "Over there," he said, pointing. "Do you see it? It's behind the other albatross now, but it's an albino. We'd better get it. I've never seen one before."

They separated a little and moved toward the bird; it was Doc who shot it. It was a beautiful thing, and after Geordie had plugged the bullet hole with cotton they took it back to the warehouse, for they didn't want to leave it and it was too heavy to carry very far. After they had left it they went north, shooting rabbits as they went, cut around the northern end of the lagoon and looked in at the frigate bird rookery. A few of the males were on the nests.

"They've got eggs, all right," Doc said. "The males do most of the incubating. We might as well get a couple of sets now, while they're fresh and easy to handle."

"Maybe the eggs will be easy to handle, but how about the birds?" Geordie asked. Having watched the frigates' bold and piratical tactics in the air he wasn't at all sure that he wanted to get anywhere near their strong hooked beaks; it seemed to him that it would be safer to expose himself to a lunatic with a meat cleaver.

"Oh, they're all right," Doc said, and pushed himself into the scraggly bushes alongside of one. The bird looked at him, but didn't offer to demolish him; he ran his hand along the nest, eased it under the bird, and came out with the egg. He did the same with another one, while Geordie stood by apprehensively waiting for disaster. Doc came out of the bushes.

"Two are enough," he said. "They're usually very mild mannered, but a little uncertain. I was ready to dive at the first movement." He grinned. "The Polynesians used to use them like carrier pigeons," he said, as they walked off. "They'd tame young ones, take them off in canoes or whatever, and turn them loose when they wanted to send a message home. The blamed things would fly home and sit on their accustomed perch. They're pretty sedentary, as a matter of fact, although you wouldn't think it to watch them. They're perfectly happy to sit on a perch if they get fed once in a while. Seems strange for a bird that's so terrific in the air. Not even hurricanes seem to bother them. They can still sail around under perfect control when everything else has been driven down on a beach."

"I still don't think I'd do what you did."

"Well, maybe it would be just as well not to. If you ever want eggs, it would be better to get them at night. The birds go into a stupor then."

They shot rabbits all the way back to the cottage, and Geordie helped Doc blow the two frigate eggs and went out again with the shotgun. He shot a red-backed sandpiper, the first one they'd seen, and found a dead young Laysan albatross which he decided to take back and skin. He was halfway up the island by that time; the sky had begun to cloud over, and he decided to go back. He had enough to keep him busy for the evening, anyhow, and as a storm seemed to be coming up and the rising wind had a cold edge to it he didn't want to be caught out and soaked. By the time he reached the cottage the wind had risen to half a gale and was still increasing; the blowing sand was extremely unpleasant, and just as he reached the cottage the end warehouse, which they hadn't used because its condition was worse than the others, blew down.

After the storm had blown itself out they found that the toll of birds had been considerable; many young albatrosses had been smothered and covered or half covered by the shifting sand, the losses among the petrels was incalculable, for they had been caught in their burrows and covered up, and all of the ground nesting birds had suffered severely. It would have been worse if it had happened later when the Christmas Island shearwaters and more sooty and gray-backed terns were in, and Geordie mentioned this.

"Yes," Doc said, "you're right, but remember that this isn't the last blow we're going to have. The young gonies will be better able to stand another one later, but I doubt anything else will. When it's all said and done, it could be that the rabbits killed more birds than the feather hunters managed to kill. Let's take a walk around the island, and see what we can pick up. We haven't been very far yet."

He took a rifle and Geordie took the shotgun, and they started out around the south end of the island. A pair of mallards jumped off the freshwater pond and Geordie got them both. After he had retrieved them they both stood looking at the two ducks, of a species so numerous and familiar at home, and both their minds jumped back to the prairie marshes, the good times they had had there, and their families and friends so far away. There was a long moment of silence, which Doc finally broke.

"They make me a little homesick," he said, "but it won't last very long. I've spent so much time in so many places that I really don't have a home any more, and I suspect your life will be that way too." He smoothed the drake's feathers. "I don't know whether our interest in birds has made us like this, or the other way around. These birds might have come from Alaska or the Siberian side. Why didn't they just migrate south a little when winter came, and stay? Where have they been? What are they doing way out here? Do they interest us because they furnish endless speculation, or, like us, are they fiddle-footed and just want to see the world and do we feel drawn to them for that reason? If I knew the answers I'd know more about myself, for I think the mallards' basic reasons and mine are pretty much the same. I never was a mechanist, thank God." He paused, and shook his head. "I don't know why I went into all that, except that the fix John is in stirred me up."

"Is he better?" Geordie asked.

"He seems a little better," Doc said. "He does have a little palsy and occasional cramps, and pain in his arms and legs, and I hope he gets over that. We gave him emetics and we washed him out as well as we could after you found him, and we're keeping him warm and giving him a lot of water and some diluted milk of magnesia to help him get rid of the stuff. There's not much else we can do, except keep him away from arsenic from now on. I'm sure now that he already had a mild chronic case and then suddenly got too much somehow. He must have spilled it on a sandwich and not noticed that he did it, or something of the sort. In a day or two we can begin to feed him with stuff that's easy to digest. We'll just have to wait and see what happens."

"I feel as though I ought to be doing some of the nursing, that I ought to give you and Cap a hand. It doesn't seem right that I'm here and don't help."

"We've been over that," Doc said. "There's no use in going over it again. I think I'll take the ducks back and spell Cap for awhile. You go on, and when you get back we'll take a swim."

They parted, and Geordie went on. It seemed to him that a great many more gray-backed terns had come in from the sea, and he thought that soon they would nest. There were many more fairy terns, too, and they seemed to like the southern beach. The gray-backs were more numerous not far from the pond; they were pretty things with their black caps, the black lines through their eyes, and their pale underparts standing out against the blue sky. They were friendly and curious, and dove at him until he got away from the vicinity of the pond. A little above the beach he hunted around and found where two fairy terns were nested; he gently moved the birds and took their eggs, for Catton hadn't collected any. He knew he would have to collect several pairs of the terns sooner or later, but decided to wait.

He went on, cutting up toward the lagoon, and as they didn't have a surplus of shotgun ammunition he only shot at rabbits when he found several of them together. Near the lagoon he stumbled across a tropic bird's nest, under one of the scaevola bushes. Both birds were there, one of them on the egg and the other sitting closely beside. They didn't leave the nest but started a harsh screaming, and as he had to get another pair sooner or later he pulled them off and killed them both, and took the egg.

Collecting the migrants was like hunting birds at home, but this was somehow different. The island birds, tame and unwary, seemed more like friends than specimens and the tropic birds, both in themselves and in their flight, were beautiful. When the pressure he had applied to their breasts had stopped their hearts he stood holding them for a moment, as though waiting for his own reaction, and was surprised when he didn't have one. He had already subconsciously made the adjustment after Doc had told him to collect, realizing that the birds were needed as specimens and that science would put them to good use; they wouldn't be wasted.

He was pleased that he had arrived at this point, that he didn't feel as though he had betrayed or uselessly killed them, and went on. Around the shore of the lagoon there were a few dead young white gonies which had died since the storm; probably their parents had abandoned them. He picked up a couple of them and took them along, turning back toward the cottage because he thought that he and Doc had enough to handle with the things he was bringing in and the two mallards.

Geordie and Doc were kept very busy in the afternoons and evenings with their skinning and preparation of skins; the fact that they weren't nearly so expert as Catton drove them to taking extra pains, which meant extra time. This work, and the collecting they had to do, cut into their rabbit shooting, and although Catton's condition slowly improved to the point where they had to spend little time with him and Cap could lend a hand, their bags diminished. In addition to this the rabbits had gotten very wary. From record days in mid-January when they sometimes had killed two hundred or more rabbits they dropped down, on their worst days, to six or so, and for several weeks their average stood at about twenty-five a day. By the middle of February they had totaled about four thousand rabbits, which wasn't enough.

Presently Catton was well enough to be up and come to the table for meals, but he still had a slight palsy and it was distressing to watch the trembling of his hands. His legs hurt him, he often had headaches, and although he didn't say so he had trouble with his eyes. This was evident when he got into the bright sunlight, for he squinted and shielded his eyes. These manifestations were bad enough, but Cap said they would probably diminish with time; what concerned them more was his mental condition, which seemed to have deteriorated. He forgot things easily and occasionally fell into childish rages over trifles; this sort of thing threw a pall over their once pleasant meals and they always had to be ready to soothe him, but it was bearable so long as he stayed in the cottage or sat inertly on the steps. It was when he began to move about a little more that their troubles multiplied. His first appearance in the warehouse gave them an indication of the future.

Late one afternoon Geordie and Doc, who had been out shooting rabbits and catching rails, had also collected two fairy terns and brought them back to skin. They had put their rails into the pen and were at work on the terns, whose feathers came out very easily and consequently made them difficult to work on, when they heard footfalls with a curious flopping quality behind them. They knew at once it was Catton, for Cap was fishing and Catton still didn't have complete control of his extremities and dropped his feet flat; they glanced quickly at each other and stopped their work but didn't turn around.

The footfalls stopped immediately behind them and they could hear Catton's quick breathing. "Continue, continue," he said. "If you call that skinning a bird in Iowa, don't let me interrupt you."

Doc turned around. "Hello, John," he said, and Geordie could hear that he was being careful with the tone of his voice. "I know we're not very good, but we're doing the best we can. While you've been under the weather, we've been trying to fill out your collection."

"A labor of love, you might say," Catton remarked.

"In a way," Doc said. "You have a list to fill out, and maybe you won't have time now to do it all yourself. I know you'd have done the same for me, if I'd gotten into trouble."

"Would I?" Catton asked, and then there was a silence. Geordie sat, tense, and knew somehow that they were on the edge of a crisis; Catton would either accept what Doc had said or reject it, and if he did that it was impossible to predict what would happen. "Yes," he said finally. "Yes, I think I would help you. I'll help you now." His hand came down on Geordie's shoulder, and Geordie couldn't help a start. "Don't do that," Catton said, with the beginning of a roughness in his voice. "I'm not a leper. Move away."

Geordie very carefully slid out of his chair, and Catton sat down. He picked up a scalpel, and concentrated on the tern. He began to skin it, and despite the trembling of his hands the precision and delicacy of his work was remarkable.

Doc gave Geordie a sidewise look that seemed to indicate that Geordie should leave. "You don't need me now," Geordie said. "I'm going to shoot rabbits."

"Go shoot them," Catton said, without turning. "Earn your keep." As Geordie turned away he heard Catton say to Doc: "You can go too."

Geordie paused at the door; Doc slid out of his chair. "Good," he said. "I'll go shoot some too. Stay away from the arsenic, John. We need you too much.

He crossed to the door, and he and Geordie went out. After they had walked out of earshot of the warehouse Doc said: "Whew! I felt as though I was walking on eggs. I'll have to get that arsenic out of there when he's not around. Before he got into that, we usually knew what to look for from him, but now I don't think we do. It's going to be a little ticklish."

TWENTY ONE

Now they had a few days free from trouble, for Catton settled down to skinning birds, moving between the cottage and the warehouse and going nowhere else; he was quiet, withdrawn, and remote, as though they were all shadows to him. Doc or Cap would frequently make a quietly complimentary remark to him and he would look at them expressionlessly, his eyes rather blank and showing nothing. He ate what was put before him, frequently spilling his food because of his trembling. His mind seemed concentrated on the skinning of birds, and once in awhile they noticed that he would make the motions of skinning something when he thought that he wasn't observed; they were careful to avoid the appearance of watching him.

His apparent disinclination to go very far from the cottage and the fact that he was doing most of the skinning freed the rest of them from this chore and they were able to move about more, but either Doc or Cap arranged to look in on him frequently.

"I've moved the arsenic," Doc said, "so I don't think he'll get at it, but we don't want to leave him alone for too long. This concentration of his and the way he looks at you make me uncomfortable."

Geordie was away from the cottage as much as possible. He was very glad to be freed again, not only from Catton's depressing presence but because their time on the island was growing shorter. He had many birds to collect, and new birds were coming in. From the one or two masked booby nests that he had found earlier the total had now grown to thirty or so, mostly along the eastern side of the island. Two of the early eggs in one nest had hatched, producing ugly, naked, slate-colored creatures so voracious that probably only one would survive. Geordie got good pictures of them, and the older birds as well. They were heavy-bodied white birds with black wing edges and a black-bordered tail, and had always engaged him because their dark beaks and eyes and the black under their chins made it appear that their faces were thrust through white hoods. They were nested on the ground practically among the frigates that victimized them, which never failed to astonish Geordie, although he realized that the frigates couldn't get down through the bushes at the young, which they certainly would have eaten.

Christmas Island shearwaters, black, petrel-like birds that nested in burrows like the petrels, were beginning to come in, and Geordie collected a few of the early arrivals from under the bushes in the frigate bird colony. Like the petrels, the shearwaters weren't active during the day but flew about at night. Within a few days the eastern shore was full of them, and shortly after that they were all over the island. They wouldn't nest for several weeks, but as the colonies built up they became extraordinarily vocal, moaning, squawling like fighting cats, and flying about in the night.

They were followed by the first sooty terns, white-breasted birds that were dark above, with dark caps. They, also were largely nocturnal, appearing in the early mornings and late afternoons, noisy with their "wide-awake!" cries, flying about but not landing, apparently spending their days and nights at sea. Geordie shot the first two he saw, and brought them in.

"They never seem to sit down," he said to Doc.

"They'll sit down later, probably about the time we leave," Doc said. "They nest later, and I don't think we'll get any eggs. They're probably the most numerous birds here, when they all get together. They'll fly around and around, huge clouds of them, and go away and come back; and then one day one bird will come down and the rest will pour down after him like the snow falling in a blizzard, and then they'll nest. If they get here before we go you won't be able to hear yourself think."

"I'd like to see that," Geordie said.

"You'd remember it the rest of your life. There are so many of them that they look like a tornado whirling around. I think you'll have a chance to see it."

There were so many things to see, so many pictures to take, and so many specimens to collect that Geordie was constantly on the go. A good deal of the time he was with

Doc or Cap, for they had started their organized rabbit hunting again, but they couldn't bring their average up enough to suit them. Doc had found the first Laysan finch's nest with eggs in it, and the other small birds would probably nest soon; as they wanted a few eggs of each species they spent a good deal of time searching for them. Geordie noticed that the throat sacs of the male frigate birds had gone down, now that the eggs were laid and being incubated, and he missed them; they had been an exotic touch of color in a landscape that didn't have very much.

He spent much less time with the gonies now, for the old birds were at sea for longer periods and he had a collection of pictures of them; they had lost their novelty in any event. There were too many other birds to photograph and collect, as they came in, species by species, from the ocean. It seemed that they had arranged it among themselves not to nest all at once. He took more and more of an interest in photography, and as Doc had misplaced the other camera, just as Dr. Black said he would, he spent more and more time taking pictures.

"Maybe we could borrow Catton's camera," he said to Doc one day. "He brought one."

"He's hidden it somewhere, blast it. I hinted to him the other day I'd like to borrow it, and he just looked blank. You're doing fine, you're getting better all the time. You don't know how lucky you are that they invented something beside that ponderous big black box we had to haul around and always use a tripod with just a couple of years ago."

"I'd feel better if we had another one," Geordie said. "If anything happens to this one . . ."

"I don't want to stir John up," Doc said. "Every day that he's as quiet as he is now is a gift from heaven, and I keep on feeling that it won't last. He went off for a little while today. Cap said he went down to the freshwater pond, and sat there looking at the teal. He's got some sort of bee in his bonnet about them."

"Did he take a gun?" Geordie asked, suddenly feeling a hollow sensation in his stomach.

"No," Doc said. "Cap hurried back before he did, and hid them all. I'll show you where they are. Try not to let him see you with one."

"What does he think when we bring the dead birds in?" Geordie asked.

"I don't know. Maybe he doesn't think about it. We've had the arsenic away from him for some time now, and he doesn't seem to think of that. Want to go for a swim?"

"Yes," Geordie said. "I feel as though I haven't had a swim in a long time." He looked down over the sea, and saw that the tide was lower than it had been since they had come to the island. "The reef is almost all exposed. Doc, why don't we explore the reef?"

"Well, why not? We may not have another chance, and we've worked hard enough to take a few hours off. I'll pass the word to Cap. Maybe he'll come along too."

They had a fine time swimming and exploring the reef, and followed it until the tide began to come in again, finding a number of sea urchins and all sorts of interesting things. There were a great number of shells that they hadn't had a chance to collect before, beautiful cowries and many others, and they were well loaded down by the time they were ready to come out of the water. They had had such a pleasant afternoon and had felt so carefree that they were in high spirits when they got back to the cottage.

Catton wasn't around, and Cap decided to walk down toward the freshwater pond to look for him. Doc and

Geordie took two rifles from the hiding place and went north on the island between the height of land and the beach on the western side to shoot rabbits until it was time to prepare dinner. They had better luck than usual, which pleased them, and by the time they had gotten about as far as the northern end of the lagoon they were running short of ammunition.

"We'll have to get into the other box," Doc said. "I think I'll go back, and poison a few skins if Catton isn't back yet."

Geordie went with him for a way, and then decided to visit the lagoon. He wanted to see if any more shorebirds that they hadn't collected had come in during the day. He cut off to the east and began to climb the slope; the sun was dropping low and the sooty terns were in the air in whirling flocks. Their numbers had increased considerably and their "wide-awake!" cries seemed to come from every direction. Geordie paused and watched them for a time, and noticed several tropic birds as well; they had also increased in numbers within the last few days. One flew past not far from him with its quick and steady wingbeat, and the declining sun gave it a little added color. It was one of the most beautiful of the sea birds and he wished he knew it better, but he didn't think there would be very many of them on Laysan any more for they liked to nest in rather heavy cover and were such true wanderers of the ocean that they could move about until they found a place that suited them. He wondered how many birds had made a choice and moved away to other, more hospitable islands during the last few years as the vegetation on Laysan had declined and how many, like the petrels, had returned by instinct alone, only to be decimated by the drifting sand.

What degree of choice did birds have, how much of their choice was dictated by ancestral memory, instinct, and how did this vary by species? Perhaps they varied individually as much as people. Geordie suddenly recalled Doc's remark that the basic reason he and birds did some things was the same, and found that he was startled by it. Most of the talk he had ever heard had put people far above the rest of creation and separated them from it because, it was thought, people arrived at their decisions by a process of logic, while the animals were controlled by various instincts. He turned this over and over in his mind as he stood on the slope and realized that he had never quite believed it.

He remembered listening to the arguments of the young mechanists at the University and walking away from them to go to the library and learn about the habits and personalities of animals and then get into the sun and air. The sun and air had been the most important thing then, but now he was aware that he was here because of his feeling of kinship with the animals. This feeling, and the observations he had made because of it, had brought him close enough to them to realize that their reasons for doing things were the same as his own. Human motivation could be explained by animal behavior; if he could show people this, if he could make them realize it, it would help them to understand themselves. Maybe this had been his goal from the beginning and he hadn't realized it, but now he did. He had made a step. It wasn't a very big one and he had many more to make, but it was a beginning.

He came out of his abstraction and heard the cries of the terns again; the sun had dropped lower and they were beginning to go out to sea. He felt that he had grown a little; he straightened up and began to walk again. His head came over the top of the slope, and the first thing he saw was a figure down on the portulaca flats between himself and the lagoon, standing with one arm raised high among the albatrosses. It seemed to be posing, or making a speech; its attitude was so strange and unlikely that Geordie stopped at once and stared at it.

It was Catton. His shadow lay long before him among the white birds, which were largely ignoring him. Catton's arm dropped, his head fell forward for a moment; almost at once he raised it again, and threw both his arms up. He half turned, and Geordie could see his mouth opening and closing but couldn't hear what the man was saying.

A cold shiver ran up Geordie's back and for a moment he was unable to move; then a violent urge to escape freed him, and he turned and ran down the slope toward the sea. He was almost in the water before he stopped. He was panting and a sort of cold horror had hold of him; he was shivering, and with the vast empty circle of the sea before him he had never felt so alone. He stood a moment with his legs twitching as though they were, without his own volition, going to carry him on; he looked back to see if Catton had followed him, had seen his movement and come after him. The skyline was empty, and this calmed him.

He got hold of himself. After all, he hadn't been threatened; he had seen a madman making a speech to the unheeding birds. It had aroused a primal fear in him, it had been like a sudden confrontation with the powers of darkness, but that was past now. What should he do? The man needed help; should he go to Catton and lead him home? His quick reaction to that thought showed him that such a thing was impossible, that he couldn't do it. He started to run down the beach.

He was in sight of the cottage when he saw, in the distance, Doc and Cap hurrying up the slope toward the lagoon. He turned toward them, and then they saw him and stopped. He ran up to them, so out of breath that he was unable to talk, but Cap said: "Nod your head. Have you seen Catton?"

Geordie nodded, and pointed back the way he had come. He took several more sobbing breaths, and then could speak. "He's on the flats. He's preaching to the birds."

"He's what?"

Geordie's breath steadied. "He's making a speech to the birds." He showed them, using the wide gestures that Catton had used. "I came over the rise, my head did, and he was down on the flats. He scared me, and I ran down to the ocean, and then came here."

"Good Lord," Cap said, and looked at Doc. "I'll go get him. You two go back."

"I'll come along," Doc said. "You may need help. Geordie can—"

"No," Cap said. "It's got to be done this way. I understand this sort of thing better than you do." He raised a hand to them, and went off.

"Geordie," Doc said, "I've got to tell you something, and it might as well be now. Most of the arsenic's gone."

"Gone?" Geordie asked.

"I don't know when he did it," Doc said, "or how he found it, but when I dipped into it today, after I left you, I found that there was some arsenic on top but that the rest of it was sand."

Geordie stared at him.

"He's hidden it somewhere," Doc went on. "We'll have to throw away any food that's open, any food that can be contaminated. We'll do it right now. Come on."

Geordie followed him to the kitchen, with a gathering hollowness in his stomach as he realized that what Doc had really said was that they might all be poisoned; perhaps they had already eaten some of the arsenic. "Doc, do you think—" he began.

"No," Doc said. "It wasn't that way last night. Here.

You take this and this and I'll carry the rest and we'll take it down to the beach."

He gave Geordie half an armful and they walked down to the sea and threw everything in. The backwash took it, and carried it out.

"Now," Doc said. "Leave nothing open or lying about and don't use anything except unopened cans or meat you've brought in yourself, and don't leave the kitchen unless somebody else is there. Maybe he just got some inexplicable notion to hide it and maybe it was more than that. I doubt we'll ever know, but now we're prepared for anything. Let's go back."

"All right," Geordie said. "What will we do now?"

"We'll play it by ear," Doc said, and they walked back to the cottage. As they came around the corner Cap and Catton were just coming in. They were walking together calmly enough; there was no evidence of trouble. Catton looked at them with no change of expression, and he and Cap went into the cottage.

Presently Cap came out again and joined them. "He's tired," Cap said. "He's gone to bed."

"Where did you find him?" Doc asked.

"Walking south on the flat, coming home. He even pointed out a redbacked sandpiper among some plover, and said there were only one or two records of it in this territory and hoped someone would collect it. He didn't seem to be interested in collecting it himself. That gave me a chance to say that I doubted we'd get enough specimens to fill out his list because the arsenic was running short."

"And?" Doc asked.

"He shook his head and said: 'Too bad, too bad.'" Cap was silent for a moment. "There's the question of the water. We'd better drink as little as possible until it rains again. Beginning now, we'll have to keep a watch on him all the time. Maybe we'll find out where the arsenic is. I've rigged a hidden string to his door to wake me if he leaves his room at night. Ah, me. It's only a couple of weeks until the ship comes back, and I hope we can keep things quiet until then."

"Amen," Doc said.

TWENTY TWO

A strange time began for them. It was at first, as Doc put it, like living on the slope of an uncertain volcano and being constantly prepared to spring into action. "Not that it's that simple," he went on. "When the volcano lets go you only have to jump and run. Here, if you have to jump, you don't know what's coming next."

This expressed the situation very well; a feeling of uncertainty and tension hung over them. They quickly fell into a routine of surveillance, spelling each other on a schedule, and for several days no one went very far away. Meals became somewhat of a problem, and weren't very tasty; wastage was greatly increased, and Geordie began to wonder if the supplies would hold out. Presently the tension relaxed a little, for Catton remained quiet and didn't go very far from the house; he skinned the few birds that were brought in and did little else but sit on the ground near the warehouse and look over the sea. Then a two-day stretch of bad weather kept them all from moving very far. It was rainy and cold, with high winds, and the burrowing birds suffered again; when it was over there were numerous dead petrels around, and the shearwaters were saved from a similar fate only because they had not yet started to nest.

After the storm was over Cap and Doc suggested that Geordie begin to move around again, checking in once in awhile to keep abreast of possible developments. "Cap and I will keep in touch with each other," Doc said. "There are still rabbits to be shot, the list isn't filling out yet, and there are always pictures. There's no need for all three of us to be here all the time. We'll try to sun-dry the skins and get them into something airtight when what's left of the arsenic gives out. We've got about four thousand rabbits to date. That's not nearly enough, and we'll do the best we can with our limitations. We'd better open the other box of ammunition."

They went into the warehouse and pried the top from the remaining case of ammunition, and Geordie took several boxes out. They felt curiously light, and he opened one of them. It was packed with blanks.

"They're blanks," he said, with a feeling of having been betrayed. "Doc, they've packed this one with blanks."

Doc stared at him, and began to root through the case. He pulled several boxes out from various parts of the case and opened them; they were all the same. He threw them down in a rage, and kicked them across the warehouse. It was the first time Geordie had ever seen him

lose his temper.

"Damnation!" he said. "And again damnation! The stupid idiots must have felt the difference in weight and didn't bother to check. Oh . . ." He stood for a moment, until he was calm again. "Well," he said, "there it is. How many rounds do we have left?"

"Two hundred at the most, I guess," Geordie said, "if we rounded up all the boxes that are scattered around. Maybe Catton has some in his room somewhere, or in some of his clothes. Maybe a hundred more. We'll fail, then. We won't be able to do what we came to do."

"Yes," Doc said somberly, "we'll fail. Maybe we were meant to fail, maybe we would have failed anyhow. There are too many of them, they've got too wary, and we're too bedeviled. I said once I admired their capacity to survive, didn't I? I understand the case. I think the gods are with them, and always have been."

Geordie was too downcast to say anything, and for a long moment Doc was silent too.

"We'll do the best we can," he went on finally. "We'll cut them down until we run out of shells, and maybe we'll cut them down enough to give the vegetation a chance to come back in a measure. When we get home we'll see if we can't get the Government to send someone else out, some predator-control people, and clean them out. The only trouble is, it might take years before they do it. Bureaucrats move like glaciers, the Survey is never given enough money and has too many places to spend it; this is a remote place, unimportant to most people, unknown to them. It will be very difficult to get an appropriation, if they ever do get one. The chances are the survivors will increase again until the place is a complete desert of blowing sand, and the rabbits, the honey eaters, the rails and the miller birds will all starve together; the finches might survive because they'll eat anything, and most of the others will be diminished. You've seen what happens to the petrels and young gonies when the sand starts to blow. It will be far worse. One of the greatest nesting islands in the world will be wrecked."

He tossed up his hands. "I don't know. Maybe we were too optimistic to think we were going to shoot them all. We should have been prepared with additional measures so that if a contingency like John came up to take shooters out of circulation we would still have had traps, poison, whatnot. We should have had them anyhow. As to John, what could we do that we're not doing now? They may be able to do something for him if we get him home; if we had tied him up it might have put him into a state that would have wrecked that possibility. Cap and I talked about it, but we didn't get anywhere." He took a turn around the warehouse. "Well, you go ahead out. Shoot as many as you can, enjoy yourself, take pictures . . . Cap or I will probably join you later."

"Yes, sir," Geordie said. He got a rifle and the camera and started for the freshwater pond.

There was a good wind and the surf was high and beautiful as it broke over the reef but Geordie paid little attention to it; the blackest depression he had ever known had settled upon him. He loved the island and the things he had done and seen. And he had believed that they were going to save it. He saw now, in the light of what Doc said, that his enthusiasm had made him too naive. It was true that they hadn't been sufficiently prepared. He didn't know who was basically at fault, but that didn't make much difference now; what shook him was that men who knew far better than he what should have been done had been as naive as he. That was enough by itself, and then Catton had been piled on top of it. The feeling of apprehension that he generated, the overhanging expectation of trouble or even disaster, was constant and inescapable. He was quiet for the moment, but how much longer would he be? None of them could get away from this thought, and even the constant surveillance might relax for a moment at the wrong time.

Geordie's life had been spent among normal people; he had had no experience with an abnormality such as this, and because he had no key to it his imagination conjured up things that frightened him. Catton had never liked him, and several times lately he had caught Catton looking at him with narrowed eyes. What went on in his mind, why did he look like that?

He was approaching the freshwater pond by this time and soon he was in the midst of a great storm of sooty terns; their numbers had vastly increased in the last day or so. Their crying filled his ears and echoed inside his head, and their innumerable company wheeled around him like a whirlwind; they forced him out of his gloomy concentration. He couldn't maintain it in the midst of so much vivid, tumultuous energy, and he began to get outside himself again. When he passed the pond he saw five teal on it. One of them was separate from the others and looked puffed up and cold; he hoped that it wasn't sick or going to die. A little further on he came out on the south beach and saw that the gray-backed terns had started to nest.

There was a part of one colony that was sitting at the very edge of the water and some of the birds were hovering over it, and he realized as he watched that the wind was on shore and was driving the ocean over their nesting places. When he got a little closer he could see eggs rolling around in the backwash. The tide was almost at its high, and the thought came to him that other terns would nest there when the tide went out and he would be able to gather fresh, newly laid eggs. They could be a great help to their diminishing supplies. The urgent life around him, the sun and the wind, had taken hold of him. He took some pictures, and went along the beach. He walked to the northern point where the offshore wind was raising a splendid surf, and sat down and watched it for awhile. As he watched the great combers running in, cresting against the sky trailing plumes of spray, and crashing down in gleaming white, he thought for the first time in many days of home, and wondered what his father would have done in the matter of Catton.

He didn't want to go back to the cottage any sooner than he had to and decided to shoot rabbits until the tide was low again, when he could see if the terns had laid enough eggs to collect a dozen or so. He concentrated on the rabbits for several hours and managed to kill thirty-five of them. He finally decided he had better go back; Doc had asked him to check in occasionally. He cut across the island, and as he approached the cottage he could see Cap and Catton walking about. It was just about then that a rabbit jumped up in front of him, ran a little way toward the freshwater pond and stopped. It was a long shot, but he took it. The rabbit wasn't killed; it rolled over, got to its feet, and made a staggering run toward the two men. It was too shocked and hurt to see them and ran straight for them; it was almost upon them when it stopped. Geordie was running after it to finish it, and was close enough to see Catton start forward and put his foot on it.

He had apparently only stepped on its leg, and the unfortunate beast flopped about trying to escape him. It began to scream, sharp, piercing cries of pain and terror, and Catton began to kick at it with his other foot. He was clumsy about it, for the nervous involvement was still with him; it was a grotesque business, but what appalled Geordie was his expression of pleasure. He was enjoying the animal's distress and outcry, and he was not trying to kill it so much as to make it suffer more. Cap stood for a moment staring at him and then ran a few steps, picked up a stick, ran back, and whacked the animal on the head. It stopped struggling, Catton stepped off it reluctantly, and Cap took him by the arm and led him off toward the pond.

Geordie had stopped; he stood there, with the rabbit's screams still seeming to echo in his ears, and then saw Doc standing on the steps. They walked toward each other and met near the rabbit. Neither of them wanted to look at it.

"I wonder if he would like to have any of us in the same situation as the rabbit?" Doc said.

"Did you see his face?" Geordie asked.

"No," Doc said. "But I didn't have to. I'm not at all sure that Cap's string to his door is enough of a safeguard any more. Cap and I had better spell each other during the nights.

"I'll do it too." Geordie said. "I've been let off too much, so please don't tell me that I can't. I can stay awake a few hours, and give each of you more sleep."

"All right," Doc said. "I'll arrange things with Cap. If you hear anything at all while it's your turn, wake us both. Yell, do anything."

"Yes, sir. I guess I'd better do something about this rabbit in the meanwhile."

Geordie went to bury it before starting his preparations for dinner, for he wanted it out of sight.

TWENTY THREE

The days and nights passed in uneasy progression toward the time of KITTIWAKE's arrival, and as though in irony the weather grew even more delightful, cool and sunny; it was the beginning of the best time of year on Laysan. Thousands more sooty terns came in from the sea, and the shearwaters increased; their moanings could be heard anywhere during the hours of darkness. There were more tropic birds and fairy terns, and red-footed boobies began to nest. The gray-backed terns, as Geordie discovered, laid eggs with pink yolks; he never quite grew accustomed to pink omelettes, and wished mightily that he could make a pink cake.

During his watches in the night, when all was quiet except the shearwaters, the moans and squalls of these birds were like an accompaniment to his thoughts of protests and regret that their last days, which could have been so pleasant, were clouded by Catton's presence and affliction, by the tension of not knowing what he might do or when he might do it. Since the episode of the rabbit he had been calm enough, but it was an uneasy calmness; there seemed to be a waiting quality about it. Their lives and their work were circumscribed and limited by it and everything slowed down. They had trouble with some of their skins, for beetles got into them; meals were tasteless and lacking in variety. If any of them went anywhere it was with the feeling that they should soon be getting back, and the carefree companionship of their fishing, swimming, and exploration parties was gone.

Geordie kept busy reconstructing boxes from the old, broken boxes left by the Japanese hunters and packing them, collecting sand and grasses for Dr. Black and as many eggs and specimens as he could, and taking pictures and making notes on bird behavior. He spent as much time as he could shooting rabbits, and was joined by Cap and Doc as often as they were free. He finally found the other camera that Doc had lost on the ground below the nesting frigate birds, but the weather had pretty well finished it. He and Doc built a traveling pen for the rails, and he fished a little for the kitchen; at another very low tide he caught some crayfish with a long-handled net that he had devised, and they had a banquet. He dug out some shearwater and petrel eggs, for the petrels, which he thought had been pretty well wiped out by the blowing sand, once again seemed as thick as they had been originally.

In all these enterprises there was a pleasure tinged

with melancholy, so that sometimes they seemed to be made-work, a sort of marking time, for the joy had gone out of the adventure. The long-winged albatrosses coming in from the sea, the rakish, piratical, soaring frigates, the terns and tropic birds and all the other multitudinous winged life was still beautiful and endlessly interesting to watch, but his thoughts turned increasingly toward home and the mail that KITTIWAKE would bring him.

One day there was a little flock of red phalaropes on the beach, and he collected one of them. It was a female just coming into the bright breeding plumage, a trim, handsome little bird, of a species not well known because it spends most of its life far at sea, skimming the waves and coming down to float like a little gull at rest, migrating back to the lonely high Arctic to nest on the Alaskan tundra or in Siberia. It was a cousin to the Wilson's phalarope that he and Spence had shot, the one he had on his desk at home; and as he held it, there skirted on the edge of his mind, to be swiftly suppressed, the question of whether this was the life he really wanted after all.

In a day or two now KITTIWAKE was due, and their packing was about finished. The boxes of skins and skeletons, eggs and shells and other things they had gathered were in the dismantled workshop in the warehouse, ready to be taken to the ship. With what little ammunition they had left they shot rabbits. Geordie did more of this than anyone else, for Catton had become restless and Doc and Cap spent most of their time near him, or within hail of each other.

He roamed the island, intent on getting his last impressions of it, of fixing it all in his mind beyond any forgetting, although he knew he would never forget it. It would be in his mind forever, until the day he died: the sweep of the lagoon with its nesting flats dotted with albatrosses, the lovely fairy terns that came to hover before him like dark-eyed little disembodied spirits, the moaning of the shearwaters, the boundless sky and the boundless sea and the freedom they had had for awhile. He had a thick book of notes and a great many excellent pictures, but the color and movement and the things he had felt would be inside his mortal skull and he wanted them fixed and sure.

The morning of the day that KITTIWAKE was due the sea was rough and boisterous, breaking high on the reef; if she reached her anchorage off the island no boat would be able to make the passage. They looked for her occasionally but hadn't sighted her by lunch time, and thought the weather might have held her up. In the middle of the afternoon Geordie decided to pay a last visit to the freshwater pond, and picked up a rifle and went off. When he was near it a frigate bird that was soaring high above him slid down the air and skimmed the surface for a drink, rose on the wind and was whisked high again, black, rakish, and beautiful in its mastery of its element.

As he approached the margin of the pond Geordie saw a dark shape lying near the water, and coming up to it saw that it was a dead Laysan teal. It was probably the sick one he had noticed a few days ago; when he picked it up it was still slightly warm and limp, and had probably died within the hour. He was very sorry to see it dead, for now there were only six of them so far as he knew in all the world. At the same time he was delighted to get it; it was a treasure, for there were so few skins anywhere. He took it to the south beach, where he was able to collect twenty-three terns' eggs for supper, and turned back toward the cottage with the eggs inside his shirt.

He was so happy in his luck at finding the teal that he carried it by the legs for all to see. There was no one in the cottage and he went around to the back. Cap, Doc, and Catton were standing there, looking out to sea; KITTIWAKE had come over the horizon, and they were all looking at her. Doc turned, and Geordie held up the teal and said: "Lucky me! I found it dead."

Doc's face lighted up, and then quickly changed. His hand started to come up, to motion Geordie to silence or wave him away, but it was too late. Cap and Catton had heard Geordie speak, and they also turned. Catton stared at Geordie and at the teal, and then became very agitated.

"He shot it!" he exclaimed. "He shot it! He shot it, and all your wretched, cheating lies have come to nothing, for he brings it here for me to see! I knew it! Didn't I say? Now the ship comes in, there's no reason to wait, and now—"

His face contorted, he made a step forward, and Doc took him by one arm and Cap took him by the other. He struggled a moment and suddenly became still; hunched, hanging on the restraining arms, he looked like a trapped animal and showed his teeth.

"I didn't shoot it," Geordie said, appalled at his own foolishness. "I found it dead. It's been sick for a few days, I saw it away from the others . . ."

"It's limp, it's newly dead!" Catton said, and his voice rose almost to a screech. "Oh, liars! Oh, thieves!" He tried again to pull away, and once more gave up.

"Take it away," Doc said, and freed Geordie from the paralysis that had fallen upon him.

He ran around to the kitchen, took the eggs out of his shirt, found a sharp knife there, and ran on until he was over the crest of the rise around the lagoon. He didn't stop until he was on the flats, and dropped down. He was panting and shaking, the flats blurred on his sight, and his stomach seemed to be rising into his throat; he sat for a moment and then sprawled full length, with his head on his arms.

Presently, calmer now and filled with a sort of despairing regret at his own stupidity, he sat up again. He wondered what he should do and then thought that he would have to stay here, stay away from the cottage until the boat came in. He couldn't go back, he would have to leave Doc and Cap alone with Catton to do what they could with him now that he had aroused the man. He rocked to and fro in his distress, not knowing that he did it. "I should have known," he said. "Oh, I should have known." Then he saw the teal beside him and began to skin it, having trouble because of the trembling of his hands.

Some time later Doc found him there, sitting on the ground and staring at the teal skin in his lap. Doc sat down beside him, and put a hand on his shoulder.

"Geordie," he said. "Geordie, don't take it so hard, boy."

"Doc," he said miserably. "How could I have been such a fool?"

"Easy does it," Doc said. "We finally got a stiff shot of morphine into him, enough to knock out a horse, and he's sleeping now. I don't know whether they'll get through the reef tomorrow. We'll probably keep him under until the boat gets in. After that we'll have help, and he'll be so seasick he'll be no trouble anyhow. Come on, let's go back."

"I can't face Cap," Geordie said. "I'll never be able to face him again."

"Nonsense," Doc said heartily. "Cap holds nothing

against you. We understand thoroughly how excited you were about the teal. I'd probably have done the same thing."

"No, you're wiser than that. You'd never be that stupid, you never have been."

"Haven't I?" Doc said. "Come, get up, and let's go back. Were they tern eggs in your shirt? I'm ready for another omelette, and so are you."

When the sun went down the sea was still running high and a cloud bank lay on the western horizon; if it moved off, Cap thought, the wind and the sea might drop by morning and let the boat through the reef. "If it doesn't," he said, "the day after will probably be all right. I'll keep the needle handy, in any event, if we have to wait another day or so, but I think we'll keep watch tonight anyhow. Would you like the first one, Geordie?"

"Yes, sir," Geordie said. "I don't think I'll go to sleep very easily anyhow."

"You shouldn't feel bad," Cap said. "If you sinned at all, you made it up with that omelette. I didn't even mind the lack of salt. I'm going to sack out. Call Doc when your shift's over, and stop blaming yourself. Good night."

They said good night to him, and presently Doc went off to bed too. Geordie could hear him moving around as he undressed and he could hear the creak of the cot as he lay down on it. Quiet fell on the cottage. There was only one lamp burning now, low, and as it was a warm night Geordie presently got up and opened the door, which they had curtained to keep the petrels out. He could hear the shearwaters moaning, and after he had looked in quietly on Catton he sat down again; presently a petrel walked in the door. It walked across the floor, climbed up Geordie's leg, and sat on his knee looking at him. Then it moved up his thigh and started to scramble to his shoulder; he caught it gently, stroked it a little, and got up once more and tossed it outside into the air again.

Time passed slowly after that and Geordie, tired by the emotions and the events of the day, sat without thought, patiently waiting for his watch to be up. Finally it was, and he looked in on the sleeping Catton again, woke Doc, and went into his room. He was so tired by now that he dropped onto his cot without taking his clothes off, and was soon asleep.

Later he awoke with a start. It seemed to him that he had been dreaming, but he couldn't remember a dream; for a moment he lay listening, with a strange uneasiness. The house was quiet, but the uneasiness grew stronger, and after a moment he got up, quietly cracked his door, and looked into the living room. He had slept through Doc's turn and now Cap was on watch. Cap was sitting in a chair, facing Catton's door; he had turned up the light a little and was reading, and as Geordie looked he turned a page. He wasn't asleep. Geordie softly closed the door again, but now the uneasiness seemed stronger than ever, it ran along his nerves, and he went to the window next to the warehouse and moved the curtain aside and looked out.

For a moment he couldn't see anything in the darkness, and then he realized that there was a ghostly, disembodied, flickering sort of glow. His hair stood up, for at first he didn't connect it with anything and in his condition thought at first of some sort of supernatural manifestation; then he thought of fire. He dropped the curtain and moved quickly out into the living room, and Cap heard him and looked around.

"Cap!" he shouted. "Cap, something's happening out there!"

He didn't finish, because Cap stood up quickly and went to Catton's door. He opened it, and whirled around.

"He's gone!" he said. "Come on!"

They ran out of the house. There was no front on the warehouse, and as they came before it they could see the fire in the loose piles of dried grass they had gathered to stuff around boxes and things in their packing. It was already beginning to catch on the board walls.

"We'll have to get the boxes out," Cap said. "Get Doc."

Geordie ran into the cottage and through Doc's door and shook him awake. "Fire!" he said. "Fire in the warehouse!"

Doc jumped up and they ran out together. The fire was brighter now, and Cap had found a shovel and was throwing sand over the boxes and scattering the straw; the old dry planks of the wall were beginning to blaze. "The boxes!" Cap shouted at them. "Get the boxes out!"

Geordie and Doc ran into the fire, dodging the blazing straw and kicking it away, and began dragging the boxes out. They worked like madmen, dodging each other and Cap, now in the darkness and now in the firelight, gasping and tugging and stumbling about in their anxiety to save the boxes, and as Geordie ran back in from one of his trips he saw a figure suddenly appear and grapple with Cap and then he saw Doc running up and fell it with a blow.

"Get hold of him!" Doc shouted, and stooped to get his hands on the figure's head. Geordie ran up and felt around in the flickering light for the feet, and they lugged their burden out into the darkness and ran back.

This lost them the last two boxes, for while they were carrying Catton out the fire had progressed too much for them to go in again. They gave it up and withdrew a little and stood together, spent and gasping, sweating and begrimed and black like three infernal figures resting a moment from their demonic labors. The roof had caught fire, and the light from the mounting flames caught at the pale undersides of a few petrels that passed or hovered and seemed like minor demons flitting by.

"Pretty soon the house will begin to go too," Cap said. "We'd better save what we can out of it." He felt his pockets. "My needle," he said. "It's on the table. I'll get it and give him another shot. Stay with him until I get back, and then we'll get what we can out of the house." He turned and trotted off toward the cottage.

The sky began to pale, and in the wan, strengthening light they sat on the ground, leaning against boxes, and wearily contemplated the smoking ruins of the cottage and the warehouses. Soon the birds that took their prey at sea—the squid that came to the surface during the hours of darkness—would be off, to return after their hunting, and the day birds would begin to stir. Cap sat nodding a little way off beside Catton, over whose recumbent figure he had arranged a blanket. Half an hour earlier he had joined them for a few minutes and talked about Catton. "I don't know how he woke from the shot I gave him," he'd said, "or how he got out. I had to go out front for a minute or two, and maybe he crept out then and hid beside the door. It was pretty dark, but I thought I was watching all the time. I looked in on him just before I went . . . I'm sorry, but it doesn't make any difference now."

"None of it makes any difference now," Doc had said. "We could have tied him up or knocked him on the head and tossed him into the sea, but we're men of good will. How could we gauge him? He's lost in a maze we lack a map for, and I'm glad nothing worse happened. We've got most of the boxes, and that's the important thing. Don't blame yourself, man."

"Thanks for those kind words," Cap had said, and gone back to Catton again.

Geordie hadn't said anything. Cold and dispirited, worn out by the past day and the night, he had been wrapped in his own thoughts and depressed by the questions within him. He sat silent for awhile longer, shivering a little, ranging far back through the years and the things he had done and thought, and his efforts to find a way for himself; he thought of his father and how well Alfred Sutton had been able to control *his* life and how totally unable he seemed to control his own. He looked at the burned and smoking ruin in front of him and then around the island in the gathering light. It was flat and sandy, soon to be sandier still, a desert of blowing sand and a ruin itself, and revulsion filled him.

"Doc," he said. "Doc, I'm going to be a lawyer."

Doc turned a grimy face, and looked at him for a long moment. "So," he said quietly. "Go on."

"Doc, I love this life," Geordie said, beginning slowly, trying to say what was in his heart, for he owed Doc a great deal, "but there are too many things about it that can't be controlled. At almost every point the success of what we set out to do depended on someone else, and at almost every point they let us down. And now that we've failed it will probably take too many years, as you've said, for the bureaucrats to get around to doing anything so someone else can fix it. Doc, there are too many disinterested people that everything depends on for it to work. I don't think I could stand it, I'd finally get discouraged and give up, and then there would be nothing. It would be awful to know that you'd wasted your life."

He fell silent and looked at Doc beseechingly, as

though asking him to understand, and then dropped his glance to the sandy ground.

Doc didn't say anything for a time. "Yes," he began finally, in a quiet tone. "You've got it all there. It might even be worse than that. It certainly has this time, and it may be again. It's almost sure to be this way again, sometime or other."

He stopped and looked at Geordie's face, but it seemed closed and unresponsive to him. He wondered what to say next, or what to do. Ever since Geordie had found the carriage and saved his life in the blizzard he had watched and loved the boy like a son, and he knew that in Geordie's present mood he might make a decision that would waste his life. *Ah, the young,* he thought, *who would go through that again?*

Just then two honey eaters, obviously interested in each other, landed on the furthermost box and the slanting light gleamed on their brilliant vermilion feathers. Geordie had told him once that they were his favorite birds on the island. "Look," he said, and put his hand on Geordie's shoulder. "Look behind you."

Geordie turned and looked, and one of the birds began to sing. Geordie's eyes lighted up and his face changed; he looked quickly at Doc and smiled, and looked back again. "Oh, Doc," he said, "aren't they beautiful?"

"Beautiful," Doc said. "They'll go away in a minute and we'll go away soon, probably forever, and you can give them up. You'll give up the others too, all of them, and never think of them again except for an hour or two on Sunday afternoons on a short walk after dinner. There are so many beautiful things all over the earth, and a vast amount of good work to be done, but you'll have to give that up too."

"What?" Geordie asked. The honey eaters flew away,

flashing like little jewels in the sun, and he turned to Doc. He stared at his friend for a long moment, not really seeing him; he was looking into himself. Finally he shook his head as though to clear it. "No," he said. "I can't give it up. I can't ever give it up." He smiled.

Doc smiled back at him. "Good," he said, and let it go at that. "You know, I think the wind's dropping. In another hour or two they'll probably lower a boat."